# THE SCULPTOR'S EYE

## Looking at
## Contemporary American Art

**Duane Hanson,**
*Football Player*, **1981.**
**Oil on polyvinyl,**
**43¼″ x 30″ x 31½″.**
**Lowe Art Museum, University of**
**Miami, Coral Gables, Florida.**
**Museum purchase through**
**funds from the Friends of Art**
**and public subscription.**

# THE SCULPTOR'S EYE

## Looking at Contemporary American Art

JAN GREENBERG AND SANDRA JORDAN

**Delacorte Press   New York**

Every effort has been made to contact the original copyright holders
of the material included in this book.

Credits for photographs of works of art appear with the list of sculptures
on pages 120 to 122.
Credits for photographs of the artists appear with each photo caption.

Cover art: Deborah Butterfield, *Palma*, 1990. Steel, 76″ × 119″ × 26″.
(Photo courtesy of the Edward Thorp Gallery, New York.)

Published by
Delacorte Press
Bantam Doubleday Dell Publishing Group, Inc.
1540 Broadway
New York, New York 10036

Library of Congress Cataloging in Publication Data
Greenberg, Jan
The sculptor's eye : looking at contemporary American art /
Jan Greenberg & Sandra Jordan.
p.      cm.
Includes bibliographical references and index.
Summary: Discusses the nature, subject matter, and techniques of modern sculpture and
presents such contemporary artists as Red Grooms, Viola Frey, and George Segal.
ISBN 0-385-30902-3
1. Sculpture, Modern—20th century—Juvenile literature.   [1. Sculpture, Modern.
2. Art appreciation.]   I. Jordan, Sandra (Sandra Jane Fairfax)   II. Title.
NB198.G67      1993
709′.73′09045—dc20         92-16323         CIP         AC

Manufactured in Italy
October 1993
10 9 8 7 6 5 4 3 2 1

to Emily and Joseph Pulitzer, Jr.
J.G.

to Susan Jordan Cornell—sister, friend, artist
S.J.

---

ACKNOWLEDGMENTS

Many people helped us at various stages of this book. We would like to express our appreciation and thanks to them all.

The artists: Louise Bourgeois, Deborah Butterfield, John Chamberlain, Mark di Suvero, Viola Frey, Nancy Graves, Red Grooms, Duane Hanson, Sol Le Witt, Ed Love, Claes Oldenburg, Beverly Pepper, Martin Puryear, Robert Rauschenberg, George Segal, Richard Serra, Joel Shapiro, and Charles Simonds for generously and thoughtfully taking time from their busy schedules to answer questions and find photographs.

Richard Bellamy at the Oil and Steel Gallery; Char Hatzh at Leo Castelli Gallery; Karla Fox and Renato Denise at The Pace Gallery; Marvin Ross Friedman; O. K. Harris Gallery; Larry Rubin at M. Knoedler and Company; Diana Bulman at Robert Miller Gallery; Sissy Thomas, Lauri Thompson, and Sandy Cooper at the Greenberg Gallery; Rena Bransten Gallery; Sidney Janis Gallery; Donald Young Gallery; Paula Cooper Gallery; Linda Steigleder at Storm King Art Center; David Platzger at Claes Oldenburg's studio; Sharyn Jensen at VAGA; and Amy Hau at the Isamu Noguchi Foundation for their continued cheerful assistance in finding artists, photographs, and information.

Jeanne Greenberg, Emily Rauh Pulitzer, and Jerilyn Changar, Ph.D., arts consultant, who read the book in manuscript and made valuable suggestions.

Gael Neeson, Stefan Edlis, Lindsay Morgenthaler, Ann Beneduce, and Wendy Worth for lending a hand when we needed one.

And special thanks to our publisher, Delacorte Press, and to Kathleen Westray, the designer, for the time and care lavished on the manuscript.

**Claes Oldenburg painting one of his giant hamburger soft sculptures.**
(© Robert R. McElroy. Courtesy of The Pace Gallery)

# CONTENTS

# PREFACE

Those of us who live in cities or towns walk by sculpture every day. Often we rush past the statue in the square, the sculpture in a lobby. Like trees, streetlamps, houses, and cars, sculpture is part of the scenery around us. Most public sculpture is traditional—fairly straightforward statues in bronze or stone commemorating a famous event or person. But what about the other sculpture, modern sculpture in museums, parks, shopping centers, and galleries across the country? In this book we are going to stop for a minute and take a closer look.

Of course, understanding what we are looking at requires more than the physical fact of opening our eyes. It involves finding words to describe what we see. In *The Painter's Eye* we introduced a language of art with examples drawn from post–World War II twentieth-century painting. In *The Sculptor's Eye* we use the same language of art to talk about contemporary sculpture. In addition to the elements of art, familiar to readers of our earlier book, the ways sculptors play with space, light, scale, and proportion are given special consideration.

We interviewed artists working in as wide a range of mediums and styles as possible. These conversations are included in chapters focused on subject matter, space, and materials, as well as in individual interviews. It's exciting to discover that the vocabulary we use when we look at these works is the one artists use to talk about making art. In fact, the same vocabulary can be used to describe just about all works of art, from a painting of a Campbell's soup can to a statue of a Roman emperor.

One of the reasons we are interested in art that is being made now is that it speaks to our own lives. We have much in common with contemporary artists. Like us, they know about endangered species and the homeless, industrial waste and pollution, technology and the Holocaust. They read the same newspapers and magazines, see the same television programs, go to the same movies and sporting events, walk down the same city streets and country lanes. They were once children who went to school, grew up, fell in love. But whether their lives are dramatic or ordinary, art—making sculpture—is one of the ways they respond to and interpret the world we all share.

We asked a number of these artists about their early experiences with art as well as about the sculptures we were discussing. Robert Rauschenberg, who assembles found objects with paintings into "combines," told us that the first art he saw was paintings reproduced on the backs of playing cards. As a child with dyslexia, he found himself drawing at school rather than reading. "I always painted and drew and made things and never thought of it as a special ability. I just assumed that everyone could if I could."

While Rauschenberg's childhood experiences with art in his hometown of Port Arthur, Texas, were limited, other artists have vivid memories of early exposure to art. Mark di Suvero, who constructs strong, abstract sculpture, said:

> I first became aware of art in China, where I was born in the Forbidden City, where the spaces and courtyards and temples have an order and harmony like great music.
>
> It was in America that I took my first art classes, in the basement of a museum. My sister Lu would take my brother and myself on Saturday mornings on a bus, then walk us through a golf course to the museum art classes; afterward we would go upstairs and look at paintings. I didn't think I had much talent, and I liked the Dutch paintings best, for their clarity and sternness.
>
> Years later, when I was going to college and living in a tree house, I saw a

show of abstract expressionist paintings that had just come from New York. I thought, *This is something I can do!* It was full of life and had something in it that was sister to the wind in the trees, brother to the sea at night. So I began painting.

Making art yourself is one way to gain an understanding of form in visual images. But coming to terms with new art involves also looking and looking again—not only at reproductions in this and other books, but more importantly at the real thing.

One of the challenges we faced was trying to take in the huge variety of the intriguing and sometimes bewildering works of art we came upon as we gathered material. Before the two of us begin to write, we spend time in museums talking about sculpture together. When one of us says, "I don't get it," we go back to the basics, to the system of looking described in Chapter 1. We stand in front of a work of art trading ideas, making associations, like two gossips sharing a juicy story. At the same time we make lists of words, references, and definitions that you will find detailed in the glossary. A short historical overview and artists' biographies are also listed.

No matter how well we think we know an artwork, we find that in asking questions and finding answers, we make discoveries. One discovery has to do with the difference in our responses. Although the two of us share a vocabulary of art as well as cultural references, we interpret works in different ways. Just as each artist translates his or her feelings and ideas in a unique way, so too does the viewer. Given individual tastes and the huge variety of work available, you might ask how we settled on the sculpture reproduced on these pages. We chose works that we found sustained our interest after repeated viewings. We wanted to represent as many styles, materials, and points of view as possible.

Some of the sculptures are by established artists; other artists might be less familiar to you. Fashions in art come and go. Prices and reputations rise and fall and rise again. But the pleasure of looking survives trends, vogues, and fads. Art's enduring appeal is in the human need to communicate. Contemporary art is addressed to us and made by us. Because of that, no matter what your age or experience, as you look, you will find out you know more than you think you do. Mark di Suvero said:

Because freedom of the imagination is so important for art, it often happens that three-year-olds do better art than grown-ups. In art, freedom of the imagination is the most important act, and young people are just as good as grown-ups in this. To be able to play with colors and let what you come up with suggest the next step is to discover the wonder of making art. Later, when you grow up, the many different ways of art become revealed; it is as if you always looked at the streetlights on your home block and the lights across the street from your window, and only later when flying in a plane at night you notice that all the streetlights become one huge jewel glowing a strange message from the darkened land.

Photograph of Mark di Suvero, working on one of his sculptures. His welding mask is pushed up on his head. (Photo © Peter Bellamy)

**FIG. 1. Claes Oldenburg and Coosje van Bruggen,** *Batcolumn*, **1977. 24 verticals and 1,608 connecting units of ⅝″ x 3″ flat bar Cor-Ten steel. The inner structure is made of 2″ Cor-Ten tubing. The knob is made of 24 sections of cast aluminum welded together. The sculpture is 100′8″ high. The widest diameter is 9′9″ and the narrowest is 4′6″. The sculpture weighs 20 tons.** Located on the Social Security Administration Building Plaza in Chicago.

# 1

# WHAT MAKES A SCULPTURE?

**A** ballplayer arches high against the right field fence and makes the catch. A horse and rider jump a hurdle and, for an impossible minute, hang motionless in space. We don't have to know anything about baseball or riding to be stopped in our tracks. Our fingers tingle; we catch our breath. For one spellbinding moment all our senses come alive. We respond to works of art this way, too—the nobility of Michelangelo's *David*, the patriotic spirit of the Statue of Liberty. But not all baseball plays are memorable; not all works of art, even the great ones, produce such strong reactions. Sometimes the satisfaction comes from looking and looking again, thinking and talking about a work of art until it reveals new messages and insights.

Imagine walking down a busy city street. Turning a corner, you come upon a strange tower, a hundred feet high! Look again. It's a sculpture of an enormous baseball bat! (*Batcolumn*, FIG. 1) Traditionally, statues in public places commemorate an event or a famous person. *Batcolumn* by Claes Oldenburg might well be a salute to ballplayers or to that great American game, but in a tongue-in-cheek, irreverent way. What makes it a sculpture? What kinds of artistic skills are involved? What does it mean? In this book we will focus on these questions.

The simplest definition of *sculpture* is "a three-dimensional artwork in real space"—space that exists, not space that is depicted. A wide range of pieces crowd into that definition. From public sculpture, such as *Batcolumn*, to huge earthworks, no single style dominates the imaginations of contemporary American sculptors. Some three-dimensional works are self-contained; others interact with the environment or landscape. Some can be placed anywhere—in a gallery, a museum, or a park; others are site-specific and exist in and for a chosen setting. But wherever it is, sculpture engages us in an active experience. We view it from many different angles. For example, we can move all the way around *Batcolumn*. From the street we look up, from the building we look through, over, and down on it. Some sculpture offers us several points of view; others are designed to be viewed from the front.

At every stage, an artist makes choices.

The subject: a man or a baseball bat or an abstract form.

The material: marble or stainless steel.

The composition: scale, proportion, distortion, light, and the way the elements are arranged.

Sometimes these choices are startling, such as the size and subject of *Batcolumn*. As viewers, we tend to be comfortable with what we know. The artist pushes the boundaries, to expand the definitions of art, to give new meaning to what we already know, or to reveal something we didn't know before.

The very earliest sculptures, dating back to ancient times, were fashioned of stone, wood, clay, or metal. These weren't special art materials—they were functional, used in daily life for such items as tables and chairs, knives, storage jars, or even jewelry. Modern technology has provided substitutes for a stone house or a carved wooden spoon. Buildings as well as many household items are now made with steel, glass, aluminum, or plastic. Artists experiment with these substances to create new forms. We read the label next to a sculpture to find out what the material is. *Batcolumn* is made from Cor-Ten steel painted gray.

The medium of the sculpture often dictates how it is made. When we stand before an artwork, we wonder, "How was this done?" The three traditional methods, which are still employed today, are carving, modeling, and casting.

The artist might carve or cut away a block of stone or wood to reveal its character or the form within, using hammer and chisel or perhaps an electric drill.

Or the artist might model a sculpture out of clay, Plasticine, or wax. Most of us have handled clay or similar mediums from mud to Playdoh, so this method will be familiar.

**Photograph of Isamu Noguchi in his studio.**
(Photo © Michio Noguchi. Courtesy of the Isamu Noguchi Foundation)

FIG. 2. Nancy Graves, *Tanz*, 1984 (glass series). Bronze with baked enamel, 19" x 19½" x 10". Collection of Ann and Robert Freedman, New York.

*Tanz* (FIGS. 2 and 3) is one example of the method known as casting. Nancy Graves chooses or creates a model and uses wax to form a mold of it. Molten bronze is poured into the mold. After the metal hardens, the mold is removed. The artist then welds many of these casts together to create sculpture. Nancy Graves combines a traditional form, casting, with the more modern practice of welding. In these two views of *Tanz* we can identify an unfurled fan combined with a leafy vine welded to a

FIG. 3. *Tanz*, 1984,
SECOND VIEW.

seedpod base—a bold structure cast from delicate "found objects." The brushed-on enameled surface is painted and dripped with color, giving the piece a sense of spontaneity.

Some artists design objects that are fabricated or manufactured at a factory, rejecting altogether the traditional notion of using one's hands to carve or model a work of art. In these works, the idea or concept is considered to be as important as the finished piece.

Another method developed in this century is to use found objects. Artist Ed Love talks about gathering found objects and transforming them into *The Sweet Rockers* (FIG. 4), a portrait in welded steel of his favorite gospel singing group.

In Miami I had a large studio, part of which was filled with all kinds of raw materials and notions that my wife, Monifa, and I collected: remnants of batiks and other fabrics, snakeskins, buttons, beads, etc. Our youngest daughter, Taira, then eleven, was interested in becoming involved in the process of "costuming" *The Sweet Rockers*. Because she knew all the singers in the group Sweet Honey in the Rock, she was able to bring a certain knowledge and point of view to the process. And because of her age and who she was, she brought a certain innocence. I showed her how to operate tools such as the glue gun and told her to use whatever materials she thought best. In the beginning she was tentative, afraid she would make a mistake. Her mother and I told her that I could always go back into her work with paint and make any additions or necessary changes. Over the next few weeks, we worked to a balance of identification and nuance. Our collaboration, we all feel, was a success.

Contemporary artists use all these methods of construction and a multitude of others from sewing objects made of fabric to changing the contour of the earth itself. The artists interviewed in this book comment on where they get their ideas and how they turn them into art. Often the materials they chose, from John Chamberlain's compressed car parts to the handcrafted wooden sculptures of Martin Puryear, relate back to their childhood experiences. The techniques, form, and subject matter of artists are no less varied than life itself.

Given this diversity you might ask, "How do we talk about contemporary sculpture?" When we study any work of art we ask ourselves some questions. Most of us begin by making a judgment. "Do I like it?"

FIG. 4. Ed Love,
*The Sweet Rockers*, 1988
(from the Arkestra).
Welded steel, paint, mixed
media; height 68″ to 82″.
Collection of the artist.

For a moment let's put aside our opinions and concentrate on describing what we see. At this stage we don't need to guess the meaning of the sculpture or evaluate whether it is good or bad. Ask only, "What do I see?" "What do I know is there?" Identify the subject matter, the material, the size, and some of the sensory properties of the artwork. By sensory properties we mean what we can perceive through our five senses: qualities that are vivid in terms of touch, sight, sound, and so on. For example, what sensory words apply to the elements in *Indian Feathers* (FIG. 5) by Alexander Calder? The color (bright, not dull), the texture (smooth, not coarse), the shape (tall, not wide), the line (both curvy and staccato). When we observe the piece carefully and describe it, we are probably already talking about its various parts and the way it is composed.

**Alexander Calder at work in his studio.**
(Photo © Pedro E. Guerrero. Courtesy of The Pace Gallery.)

**FIG. 5. Alexander Calder, *Indian Feathers*, 1969. Painted aluminum sheet and stainless steel rods, 136¾" x 91" x 63".**
Whitney Museum of American Art, New York. Purchase with funds from the Howard and Jean Lipman Foundation, Inc.

**Ed Love putting the finishing touches on one of the musicians in the Arkestra.**
(Photo © Jennifer Keller. Courtesy of Ed Love.)

The second question, "How is the work organized?", is more complicated because it requires some knowledge of the language of art. The elements of sculpture, as of all artwork, are color, shape/form, texture, and line. They are the basic building blocks of art. We ask how these elements are arranged in terms of some visual effects—proportion, variety, rhythm, balance, and emphasis. These words crop up again and again when we look at art. Then we consider unity, how the elements come together as a whole.

The last and most important question is, "What is the feeling expressed?" A work of art is a visual symbol for an artist's ideas or feelings. If the various parts of the sculpture function together, these ideas and feelings can be understood by the viewer. Can the sculpture be described as playful or menacing? Does it arouse a feeling of peacefulness or tension? Soon we find ourselves asking other questions. Is the sculpture unified? Is it more or less interesting than other sculpture in this book or in a museum or at a sculpture park? What does it say about the world we live in? What do you think the artist was trying to say?

Ed Love has incorporated childhood religious and cultural experiences and images in his sculpture *The Sweet Rockers*.

Where I lived in Washington, D.C., there was an elderly man in the neighborhood who walked with a cane, a staff to which he attached different objects, ribbons, and strings. The staff changed often and seemed to be his tool for accessing the world. He always appeared to me to be a magical figure.

During this period, I was also thinking a lot about the musician Bob Marley. Marley was also taken by the idea of the rod and staff as expressed in the Twenty-third Psalm. I had learned this psalm in church as a child. According to the Bible, the rod and staff comfort, guide, and protect you from evil.

I was beginning to think about developing a series of pieces that would pay homage to magicians who have provided the audio evidence of their particular journeys and struggles. All of this,

the magic man, Robert Nesta Marley, the audio evidence of struggle, and the idea of an Arkestra (borrowed from the musical group Sun Ra's Intergalactic Arkestra), began to work on me, and I started developing figures of welded steel. The staff became an important formal element in the work. The first series was *The Wailers*. The work has since developed into a band of twenty-seven members, the latest being *Sweet Rockers*.

A great deal of thought goes into a work of art. Artists draw their inspirations from the world around them. The answer to the question "What makes a sculpture?" is not so easy. But artworks are open to many interpretations. As you look at artworks in the following pages and encounter artists discussing their work, you will begin to form your own opinions. There are no right or wrong answers, as long as you support your conclusions in the language of art. And perhaps next time you turn the corner and bump into a sculpture, you might stop and ask some of these questions or talk about it with a friend and begin a dialogue of your own.

# 2

# WHAT'S THE SUBJECT?

**W**hether an artist chooses to create a sculpture of a person, an animal, an object, or a particular form, no two interpretations of this subject will be alike. Sometimes the way an artist chooses to represent the human figure, such as the rodlike figures in *The Sweet Rockers*, is unexpected. The sculpture may be exaggerated in scale or out of proportion or distorted. It may be nonobjective, which means there is no recognizable image; it may be abstract, which means color and/or line, shape, or texture are stressed as the subject; it may be an open form stretching into space or a closed one encasing space. Artists in the twentieth century have focused on these features, as well as new materials and techniques.

Let's consider subject matter in more detail by comparing six very different pieces. They do have one thing in common; they are all interpretations of the human figure.

This bronze sculpture *Untitled, 1984* (FIG. 6) by Joel Shapiro is abstract; yet we are reminded of a figure balanced precariously in space. How do we know it's a figure? Despite the simplicity of form, the sculpture appears figural with limbs flying in four directions from the blocky torso. Suspended in motion, he is involved in a struggle, balanced

FIG. 6. Joel Shapiro, *Untitled*, 1984. Bronze, 79¼" x 78¼" x 38¾".
St. Louis Art Museum. Gift of Mr. and Mrs. Barney A. Ebsworth.

on one leg like an exclamation point. How would you move if you slipped on a banana peel or tripped on a rock? Follow the path of movement with your arms. What sensory words come to mind—*vertical*, *jerky*, *explosive*, *open*, *jutting*, *angular*? We have referred to *Untitled* as "he." If Shapiro had wanted this figure to be feminine, might he have chosen different shapes?

We identify the subject of a sculpture. Is it a man or a flower or an abstract shape? However, once we see how the elements are organized, we discover that the sculpture contains layers of meaning not immediately revealed. When we ask, "What is the expressive quality?", we are asking what the subject represents on a symbolic level. By symbolic we mean that the image conveys an idea or universal feeling. What is the symbolic meaning of *Untitled, 1984*? We will come back to this piece to uncover the answer.

We often make personal associations as we look at art. How do you react to *Football Player* by Duane Hanson (FIG. 7)? If you have ever watched a football game or played football, you may have memories—good or bad—about this sport. It may influence your response to the sculpture. But if you say, "*Football Player* is a good sculpture because I like the Miami Dolphins," the opinion, relevant to you, has nothing to do with the artwork's meaning. There is a difference between having a feeling and considering the feeling contained in a work of art. To go one step further, you might begin with "What do I see?", then move on to the formal elements of *Football Player*. How is it composed? By asking these questions, concentrating on the sculpture itself, you will discover its expressive qualities. What are the clues provided by the artist to create a scenario for the football player?

Hunkered down on his helmet, the football player, head lowered, expression grim, sits in a position of fatigue after a game. Imagine

FIG. 7. Duane Hanson,
*Football Player*, 1981.
Oil on polyvinyl,
43¼″ x 30″ x 31½″.
Lowe Art Museum, University of
Miami, Coral Gables, Florida.
Museum purchase through
funds from the Friends of Art
and public subscription.

Duane Hanson casts his figures by making molds directly on the body of live models. He makes plaster casts of various body parts, casting them with polyvinyl acetate. Then he removes the vinyl mold, and finishes the arm parts using a soldering iron. After he puts the parts together, he paints the figure using an air brush.
(Photo © Rick Webb. Courtesy of Duane Hanson)

THE SCULPTOR'S EYE

walking into a museum and being confronted by this life-size figure. Until you get about six feet away, he looks alive . . . out of context . . . but definitely life-size, with real hair, smooth skin, and a metal helmet. The illusion is perfect. His size emphasizes his realness, so much so that we are fooled when we spot him. Lost in thought, the football player is not aware of being observed. Does he look as if he just made a touchdown, as if his team won the game? Here is an American hero of heroes, the athlete, in a private moment, vulnerable, isolated, frozen in time. He becomes an archetype for every athlete in a moment of defeat.

Duane Hanson talks about his early fascination with realistic art:

> As a child I had painted, drawn, and carved figures out of wood, using my mother's butcher knives. I lived in a very small rural town in Minnesota where we had no art instruction and no exposure to works of art of any kind.
>
> Although I had seen art depicted in a few books that were available, it was not until I was about fifteen or sixteen before I saw any genuine works of art. I had gone to the Walker Art Center in Minneapolis. In those days both modern and traditional works were displayed. On the second floor was a painting of a very young pretty girl by the famous nineteenth-century French painter Bouguereau. I was totally fascinated by the haunting eyes of this girl and wondered how it was possible for the artist to create such a strong sense of reality by using a few paints and brushes. I still remember those eyes. Later on when I took some art classes in college, they informed me that realism was dead and that Bouguereau was a degenerate painter. One had to reject realism in order to become modern. This was hard for me to take seriously, but after all this time I am hearing the same thing from certain pedants.

**Scale.** One of the first things we notice about *Football Player* and this ceramic sculpture by Viola Frey, *Me Man* (FIG. 8), is their size. In other words, how does the size compare to us, to human scale? Or how does it relate to the room, the building, or even the site? The size or scale of a sculpture affects our interpretation of the subject matter.

This lustrous fired-clay ceramic piece is made of six parts that fit together. It is almost ten feet tall. Clearly *Me Man* is a male dressed in a suit and tie, but the scale is not of human size. He looms over us, larger than life. Leaning in our direction, gesturing, he's not about to say, "Have a nice day." He's an authority figure, "The Big Boss."

Remember what it felt like to be two years old standing next to an adult? What would happen if, instead of being nearly ten feet tall, the man

**FIG. 8. Viola Frey, Me Man, 1983.**
**Glazed ceramic, 99" x 29¾" x 25".**
Whitney Museum of American Art, New York.
Gift of William S. Bartman.

was only ten inches tall? His stiff posture and cranky expression wouldn't change, but our response to him might be different.

In *Trapeze* (FIG. 9) by George Segal, life is mimicked but not reproduced. This life-size figure of a trapeze artist has been taken out of the circus and placed high above our heads in the museum. Although he isn't flying through the air, we are familiar with his act and can imagine what might come next. But for now he hangs motionless, preparing for flight. Like an actor on the stage, the trapeze artist seems dramatically alive, but the white plaster separates him from real life. Still, because he is human scale, cast like Duane Hanson's figures on a live model, we identify with him. Some words that come to mind are *ghostly*, *passive*, *floating*, *mummylike*, *theatrical*, *intimate*.

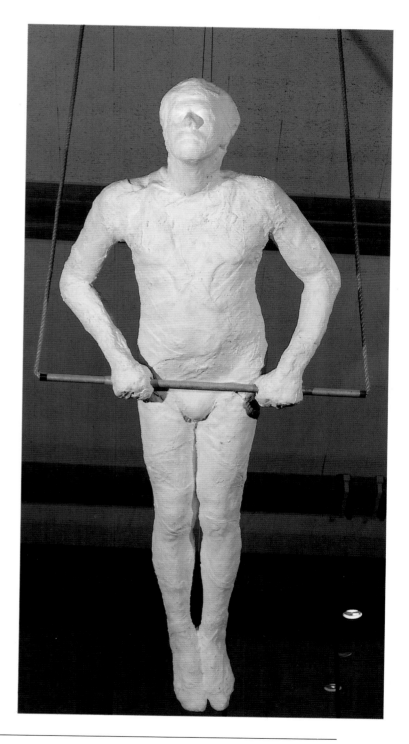

**FIG. 9. George Segal, *Trapeze*, 1971. Plaster, rope, metal, and wood, 72" x 36". Wadsworth Atheneum. Hartford, Gift of Joseph L. Schulman and an anonymous donor.**

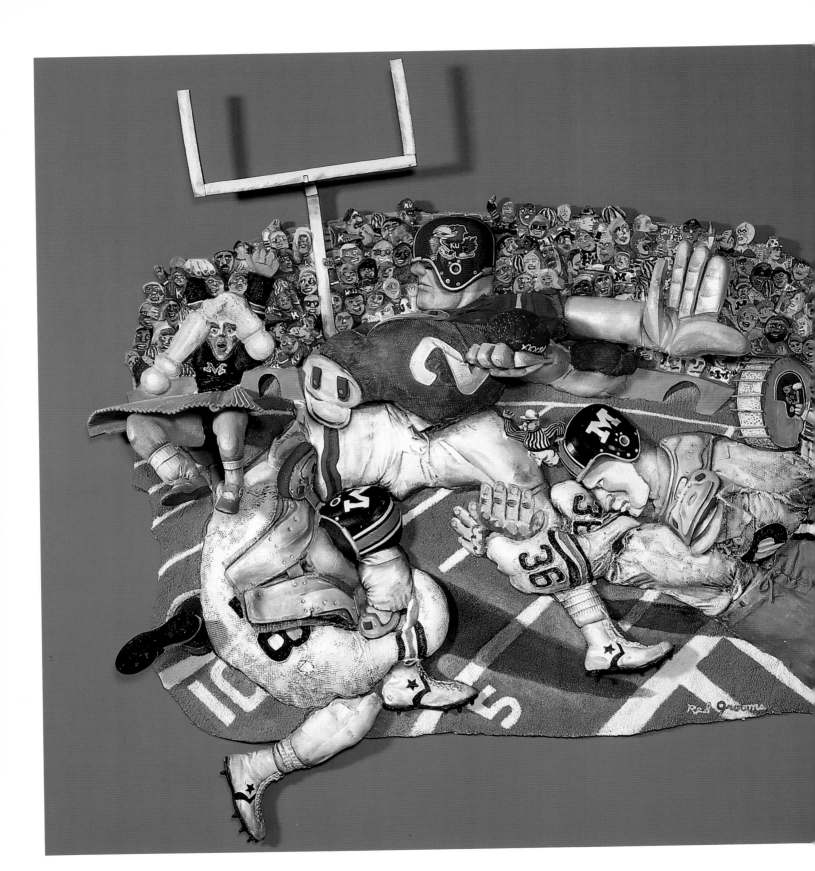

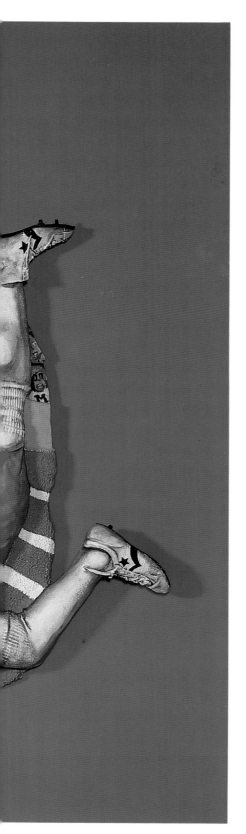

**Proportion and Distortion.**   Artists are concerned with proportion, how the various parts of a sculpture relate to each other. An unexpected shift in proportion is called a distortion. It is used knowingly by the artist for emphasis and emotional impact.

This metal relief, *The Big Game* (FIG. 10) by Red Grooms is a close-up of a tackle at the line of scrimmage. (A relief is a three-dimensional sculpture made to hang on a wall.) The figures are distorted—their torsos, legs, hands, and arms exaggerated from what might be considered normal proportions. Unlike Duane Hanson's defeated *Football Player*, these athletes are engaged in the rough-and-tumble combat of their sport. Notice the enlarged hand reaching out at top right, the tiny referee, the oversize drum, and the cheerleader leaping high in the air. Even the goalpost is askew. All these details are out of whack, giving the viewer a sense of movement, of thrusting action. Behind the game, the tiny cartoonlike faces of the spectators polka-dot the stands. By contrasting the size of the audience with the massive players, the artist achieves the illusion of depth. This raucous caricature of football dramatizes the battle, not a defeat.

FIG. 10. Red Grooms, *The Big Game*, 1980.
Painted cast aluminum, 96" x 101" x 17", edition of three.
Courtesy of United Missouri Bank Collection, Kansas City, Missouri.

Both scale and distortion affect the visual impact of Claes Oldenburg's *Floor Cone* (FIG. 11). What is this soft squashy form, slumping across the floor? It takes us a moment to recognize the distorted shape as a twelve-foot pistachio ice-cream cone. In spite of the enormous scale, the artist bases his object on human proportions. The long sensuous cone might be the body, the scoop of ice cream, the head. Or the ice cream might be a pillow, the cone a bed. The plumped-up quality of the material and the curved lines tempt us to take a flying leap and sink into it. In this humorous sculpture, Oldenburg insists that anything can be a subject for art, even fast food. He encourages us to reflect on a mundane object in a new way, to appreciate its shape and its effect on the space around it. Some sensory words are *soft*, *curvy*, *shiny*, *long*, *plump*, *squashy*.

Oldenburg wrote, in part:

I am for the art of abandoned boxes, tied like

FIG. 11. Claes Oldenburg, *Floor Cone (Giant Ice-Cream Cone)*, 1962. Synthetic polymer paint on canvas filled with foam rubber and cardboard boxes, 53¾" x 11'4" x 56". The Museum of Modern Art, New York. Gift of Philip Johnson.

pharaohs. I am for an art of water tanks and speeding clouds and flapping shades.

I am for U.S. Government-inspected art, grade A art, regular-price art, yellow-ripe art, extra-fancy art, ready-to-eat art, best-for-less art, ready-to-cook art, fully cleaned art, spend-less art, eat-better art, ham art, pork art, chicken art, tomato art, banana art, apple art, turkey art, cake art, cookie art.

I am for an art that is combed down, that is hung from each ear, that is laid on the lips and under the eyes, that is shaved from the legs, that is brushed on the teeth, that is fixed on the thighs, that is slipped on the foot.

How might an artwork be the subject matter for a poem or vice versa? Begin by making a list of common objects. Then, like Oldenburg, imagine them small or large, hard or soft. Give them a personality, a voice. If you were going to choose an object as a metaphor for yourself, what would it be?

# TALKING WITH THE ARTISTS I

## Red Grooms, Viola Frey, George Segal

Red Grooms, Viola Frey, and George Segal are American storytellers who offer us glimpses into everyday life. But instead of words, they create in three dimensions. Each employs very different methods and materials. Each has a different story to tell. "Where do you get your ideas?" we asked them.

## RED GROOMS

Red Grooms beckons us into his wild and wacky world. He presents a vision that is both realistic and a darkly comic social satire. *Looking along Broadway towards Grace Church* (FIG. 12) is full of distortion. Figures, wastebaskets, fire hydrants, signs, lamp posts, are stretched and twisted. Words that come to mind are *noisy, frantic, rushed, crowded, aggressive, bustling*. The artist has used distortion to suggest vitality and movement—we almost can hear the blare of the radio, the honking of taxi horns.

FIG. 12. Red Grooms, *Looking along Broadway towards Grace Church*, 1981.
Alkyd paint, gator board, Celastic, wood, wax, foam core, 70¼" x 63¼" x 28½".
Cleveland Museum of Art. Gift of Agnes Gund in honor of Edward Henning.

**Q.** Tell us about this piece.

**R. G.** For *Looking along Broadway towards Grace Church* my fixed point of view was on the corner of Walker Street and Broadway. It's a very short walk from my studio, so I had the luxury of going out to take Polaroids or sketch whenever my imagination started to run out of gas. I like to put real-looking facts in my work, hoping that by doing so it will be more convincing. I always get into a slight panic when confronted by the "real thing,"

**Red Grooms in 1987 working with his assistants on the *The City of Chicago*, an installation at the Whitney Museum of American Art.**
(Photo © George Hirose. Courtesy of Red Grooms)

afraid that I won't be able to get it all down, so I usually gather more information than I can find space for in a 3-D relief or painting. This was the case with *Looking along Broadway towards Grace Church*.

**Q.** You have a lot going on in a small space. How did you think about the scale?

**R. G.** From where I stood to the church was a mile of quickly foreshortening buildings. I had a two-foot depth in my relief. I needed to do a lot of compressing, so I chose to use a comic approach. In strict architectural models, space has to be rendered logically. Humor gave me the license to "gag" space up. It fit into the New York scene. Things are jumbled together there anyway. It would make no sense to straighten them out.

**Q.** What do you remember as your first real encounter with art?

**R. G.** When I was a kid, my dad told me a tall tale. Somewhere near his home in west Tennessee, he said, there was a park filled with stone sculpture of cars, boats, and airplanes. Although it was really an imaginary place, I believed it existed and had it fixed in my mind. I lived in the suburbs so I liked imagining these stone cars and things in some vague countryside. The landscape is so flat there that stone sculpture would stick out like a sore thumb. I thought they would be life-size—boats and cars all made out of stone. I liked the phantasmagorical quality of these real things made of stone. I converted that practice later in larger works. I wasn't content with imagining things. I wanted to build them myself. One of the driving forces of sculpture is to actually become physically involved with the materials.

I've always been interested in scale changes. I like my pieces to relate to human scale so you can walk around them.

In Nashville, my hometown, there's a replica of the Parthenon built around the turn of the century. My parents used to take me there. It was a tourist attraction. But I had this fear of going inside because it was a big empty room. Later, in fact, I did go inside. It was filled with reliefs of Greek sculpture, and that place had a great sculptural impact on me.

# VIOLA FREY

*Double Grandmother* (FIG. 13) is a sculpture of life-size figures in ceramic, glazed with rippling color. The two women stand like mirror reflections of each other, with their sturdy figures and dowdy clothes, holding up their gifts. "They might be grandmothers," says the artist, "but you don't feel you have to help them crossing the street, do you?"

**Q.** Why two grandmothers?

**V. F.** Well, most of us have two. I grew up in Lodi, California. Everyone who lived in Lodi was a rancher—grapes or fruit crops. The women of my childhood were strong women, energetic and powerful.

The technical difficulty of making the grandmothers was how to support the weight of the figures on the slender ankles. I solved it by firing the ankles, then firing the rest. It took me a long time to figure it out. Another problem of the grandmothers was to work in color, to be specific to a feeling, not to create a sentimental portrait.

My teacher at Tulane was Mark Rothko [the painter]. He said that whether a painting was

**Viola Frey in her studio in California.**
(Photo © M. Lee Fatheree.
Courtesy of Rena Bransten Gallery)

FIG. 13. Viola Frey,
*Double Grandmother,*
1978–79. Glazed white clay,
61½″ high.
Minneapolis Institute of Arts.

**FIG. 14. Viola Frey, *Me Man*, 1983. Glazed ceramic,
99" x 29¾" x 25".**
Whitney Museum of American Art, New York. Gift of William S. Bartman.

abstract or realistic, when he painted the color red he was painting the sensation of a red apple against a red tablecloth. I strive for that feeling in my color too.

**Q.** How did you start glazing your clay figures in color?

**V. F.** The light is different in California where I live than it is in the East. The color has a certain sparkle. Color is also about light and reflection. Even texture. And glazes are different from paint. There is more light in them. Glazes are painting on three-dimensional pieces. Of course, histori-

cally much of sculpture was in color. All those white marble Greek statues were painted. We don't think about that lately. And ceramics are also a lot about color. Again, being from the West Coast, I felt a stronger influence from the Far East, China and Japan, than New York.

**Q.** Tell us about *Me Man* (FIG. 14).

**V. F.** The size came about because the ceiling height in the studio where I was working was then eleven feet. And you could make something go all the way to the ceiling, but you had to have room to get up there with a ladder. So he is the maximum size I could achieve in that space. By increasing scale you often want to get a public size, a sculpture that relates to the space around it and the buildings rather than to a person. But in spite of his size *Me Man* was done for a human scale, in relationship to my figure, not as public sculpture. It is meant to be a personal distance. Up close he is an abstraction; you can only see part of the statue. The color is part of that. The painting on the statue forms abstract patterns.

**Q.** What was your first experience with art?

**V. F.** We didn't go to museums, but we did go to the library. Because I lived on a ranch we could get out a lot of library books at once, thirty at one time. My mother would be going to town on errands and I'd ask her to stop by the library and pick up some more books. She'd get them alphabetically. I'd say "This time bring me *F* to *Fi*." That way I had a range of subjects. I read through everything from art history to Dickens. So my first experience of art was from books.

## GEORGE SEGAL

George Segal's figures are cast in plaster from live models—in his early pieces friends and family members posed for him. He wrapped them in plaster-soaked bandages—the kind doctors use to make casts for broken bones. These hollow, lumpy figures are realistic yet set apart by their ghostlike whiteness. They convey a feeling of lonely isolation. He often combines them with real objects, in this case a traffic light and a truck grille, and arranges them to form environments or whole scenes. The effect is of a brief moment frozen in time.

**George Segal making a cast from a model, in the process of creating** *Girl in the White Wicker Chair.*
(Photo © Wendy Worth. Courtesy of the Sidney Janis Gallery)

*The Red Light* (FIG. 15), set in a niche in a museum, becomes a stage set or tableau.

**Q.** *The Red Light* is dramatic. There is an ominous quality about it.

**G. S.** I tend to avoid white walls. I have a place in my studio where I staple up black tar paper to create an environment. *The Red Light* is built on two plywood walls that are painted black. It's nighttime: a scene glimpsed and remembered. Out of the darkness I get an image—of gleaming red light, the red grille of the truck thrusting forward, looming up. The man is introverted, self-absorbed, dreaming. Thrusting forward himself in his own determination to cross the street. There's a feeling of danger, a sense that the truck may not stop. Seeming banal ordinary scenes repeated hundreds of thousands of times a day, once you start to look at them, are fraught with all kinds of associations.

**Q.** Space. How do you see the viewer relating to your pieces?

**G. S.** My teachers were all abstract painters. They resisted images from the real world; they aimed toward abstraction. And yet they spoke in humanistic terms of grand passions, trembling sensibility, feelings, and emotions. I wanted to enter the space of everyday. I wanted to enter a world that almost resembled the real world but was packed with my internal feelings, to couple the visible with the invisible. That meant entering the environment I had reshaped from the real world.

**Q.** What were your early encounters with art?

**G. S.** I grew up in the Bronx. My parents were flat-broke immigrants from Russia. I was lucky. I had teachers who sneaked me extra drawing paper and supplies. I drew pictures of my fellow classmates in elementary school—Public School 70. It had marble Corinthian columns, big marble stairs, giant reproductions of Thomas Eakins paintings everywhere. It was during the depression. My teachers were all Ph.D.'s and glad to have the job. One of them said to me, "For a nickel you can take the subway and go to the Metropolitan Museum and for free look at art only kings could look at." So I did. I was fascinated by anything to do with fine art.

FIG. 15. George Segal,
*The Red Light*, 1972.
Plaster, mixed media,
114″ x 96″ x 36″.
Cleveland Museum of Art.
Andrew R. and Martha Holden
Jennings Fund.

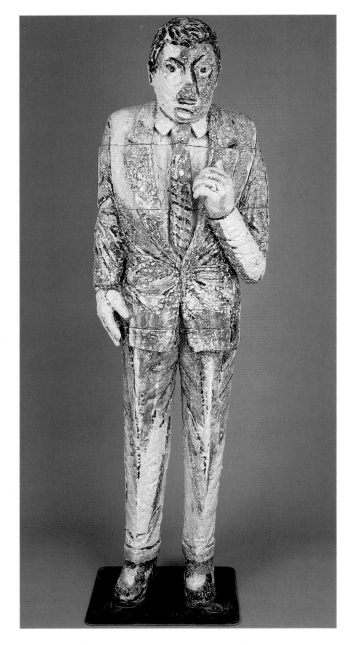

**FIG. 16. Viola Frey, *Me Man*, 1983. Glazed ceramic, 99″ x 29¾″ x 25″.**
Whitney Museum of American Art, New York.
Gift of William S. Bartman.

# 4

# SPACE...AND WHAT IS IN IT

**Q.** How is a twelve-foot fabric ice-cream cone like a white plaster trapeze artist?
**A.** They are both three-dimensional artworks that occupy real space.

The soft painted fabric *Floor Cone* stretches at our feet. *Trapeze* hangs twenty feet over our heads. No matter how innovative the sculpture, we can't talk about it without talking about space. How a sculpture relates to the space around it gives it interest and certainty as a work of art. So the language of sculpture gives us several ways to express this relationship.

Some sculpture is solid, monolithic. Visually it is self-contained. It pushes in on itself, not out into the world. An example of this spatially "closed" form is Viola Frey's stiffly gesturing *Me Man* (FIG. 16). Other sculpture pushes out toward the viewer, interacting with the space. Joel Shapiro's *Untitled, 1984*, limbs akimbo, like most contemporary sculpture, is such an "open" form.

Positive space refers to the solid parts of the sculpture—the length, breadth, and width of a work. Negative space is the void or empty space between and around the forms. A freestanding sculpture such as *Me Man* is positive space, the air surrounding it is negative space.

Here are two different photographs of this now familiar piece, *Untitled, 1984* (FIGS. 17 and 18). We have said the figure is precariously balanced in space. From one angle it looks as if he is falling forward, from another angle he is falling back. Our view of the bronze parts, the positive space, and the space that surrounds them, the negative space, alters as we walk around the piece. A feeling of tension results from these shifting relationships. The impact of the sculpture is determined as much by the spaces as by the shapes themselves.

Our point of view in a work of art, our connection with it, depends on the position from which we see it. When it is set on a pedestal, we consider it from several vantage points, but it stays separate from us. This notion of separateness has come into our language—when we say we put someone "on a pedestal," we mean setting him or her above ordinary daily life.

*Untitled, 1984* is not on a pedestal, super-

**FIG. 17. Joel Shapiro, *Untitled, 1984*.**
**Bronze, 79¼″ x 78¼″ x 38¾″.**
St. Louis Art Museum. Gift of Mr. and Mrs. Barney A. Ebsworth.

**FIG. 18. *Untitled, 1984*, SECOND VIEW.**
(These two views were taken outdoors during an exhibit at the Baltimore Museum of Art. Photos courtesy of the St. Louis Art Museum.)

**FIG. 19. Charles Simonds, *Dwellings, 1981*, DETAIL (four of eight photographs). Unfired clay wall relief, 96″ x 528″.**
Museum of Contemporary Art, Chicago. Gift of Douglas and Carol Cohen.

heroic, apart from us. The figure flails about, trying to regain his balance. We could reach out a hand and steady him. By putting us in the same space as *Untitled, 1984*, the sculptor links us to it.

The factor of time also comes into play—it takes time to explore a piece, to look at it from every angle. We can't comprehend *Untitled, 1984* in a glance. The contemplation of different views gives us a concept of the whole.

On the other hand, we peer at *Dwellings, 1981* (FIG. 19) by Charles Simonds but we can't walk around it. It is a three-dimensional relief, constructed in a niche in the wall, and our scrutiny

is limited to the front. The niche underlines the contained feeling of *Dwellings, 1981*; it has an existence removed from ours, perhaps by centuries of time as well as by space. Flat-topped buildings and low towers of tiny clay bricks rise out of rounded red-stained hills.

The style of the buildings is vaguely familiar, but the small scale suggests the archaeology of a fantastic culture, as if a diminutive race of people had built a civilization and then vanished for an unknown reason. The mysterious quality is tantalizing. We want to know more. Who was here? What is their story? Everyone's answer will be different.

FIG. 20. Mark di Suvero, *Mother Peace*, 1970. Steel painted red-orange, 39'6" high.
Storm King Art Center, Mountainville, New York. Gift of the Ralph E. Ogden Foundation.

THE SCULPTOR'S EYE

*Untitled, 1984* is in a room—or for special exhibits the garden—of a museum; *Dwellings, 1981* is set into a wall. *Mother Peace* (FIG. 20) sits in the middle of a meadow surrounded by gently rolling hills. The sculpture is unprotected, exposed to the wind and weather. The red beams, fastened by bolts and wire, jut into space. The artist, Mark di Suvero, has constructed the piece so that the upper cabled beams can move in the wind. The balance and weight of the swinging beams have an edgy feel. We approach it tentatively. At the same time the steel beams that stretch like arms across the field invite us to step inside the work, to explore the sculpture physically. It feels very peaceful to lie in the shelter of the "arms" and look up at the shifting shapes of the beams against the sky.

The piece came out of the artist's strong feelings about the war in Vietnam. He said:

> I built *Mother Peace* alone, with a crane, a torch, and a welding machine in a parking lot in Pasadena. The first upper moving part didn't say what I wanted so I did it over. It took a long time to build. I wanted the people to see that I am for peace, for life, for growth—and so I used my torch to cut the peace symbol into the beam that sways in the wind: it moves when the upper part moves. This piece of sculpture has a motion that is interdependent (we all are): the reason it exists is to give you an emotion (a special one that professors call aesthetic), a sense of openness and gentleness (it is three tons that moves slowly in the wind).
>
> I think the power to make steel into art is more important for all humans than making tanks and guns. The people who were for war and racism hated the piece because of the peace-symbol; they managed to kick the piece out of a show at the Oakland Museum. Trees, children, crops grow in peace. *Mother Peace* moves in the wind in a field in a sculpture park (Storm King) in upstate New York.

Our response to *Mother Peace* is influenced by the landscape, but the piece itself could be moved to a different location. Robert Smithson's *Spiral Jetty* (FIG. 21), a 1,500-foot site sculpture built in the Great Salt Lake in Utah, couldn't be moved. The artist used rocks and earth to create a structure on a desolate shoreline, where the only other suggestion of humanity's presence is industrial waste and oil seepage. Some associations that come to mind about the shape are whirlpools, cyclones, the inside of shells, perhaps even our inner ears. Like *Dwellings, 1981*, *Spiral Jetty* raises questions. What is it for? How long has it been here? We don't have to know the answer to want to find our own meanings—a symbol for an inner journey, a sign of our exis-

**FIG. 21.** Robert Smithson, *Spiral Jetty*, 1970. Black basalt and limestone rocks and earth, 1,500 feet. Great Salt Lake, Utah.

tence left on the landscape. This is not art for posterity, to be exhibited at a museum. You can't buy it or sell it. In fact *Spiral Jetty* has already disappeared under the rising waters of the lake. It remains only in the memories of people who experienced it and the various photographs taken at the site.

**Shape and Form.** Sculpture, no matter what the subject, is composed of shapes, forms, and lines. Consider the space where you are reading. Whether you are in your living room, the library, or outside in a field, you can see a variety of shapes. This book is a rectangle. How thick is it? What is its volume? Now look at the shape of your hand holding the book: long cylindrical fingers, oval fingernails, a square-shaped palm. Shapes are everywhere, from the curves and rectangles of your chair to the combination of shapes—square windows, four round tires, and a streamlined body—of the family car.

In *Sky Cathedral* (FIG. 22) by Louise Nevelson, a collection of boxes forms a grid of squares. Each box contains a fascinating collection of shapes and forms: circles, squares, fragmented rectangles, jagged and curved-edged icicles,

**FIG. 22. Louise Nevelson, *Sky Cathedral*, 1958. Assemblage: wood construction painted black, 11'3½" x 10'¼" x 18".**
The Museum of Modern Art, New York. Gift of Mr. and Mrs. Ben Mildwoff.

**Louise Nevelson in her studio.**
(Photo courtesy of The Pace Gallery)

arches, corkscrews, half-moons, slats, and cones. Even when we think we recognize the source of the items—a piece of gingerbread trim from a house, the leg of a chair, a bowling pin—the interest lies in the shapes themselves, not in their original function. These found objects form an assemblage and become a relief.

The shapes overlap and repeat themselves in irregular patterns and alternating rhythms. Rhythm in sculpture, which is achieved here by repeating shapes, provides movement. Artists also work with shapes, colors, lines, and texture for the visual effect of variety. *Sky Cathedral* reminds us of a church altar, a giant tool box, a dime-store counter full of tempting compartments. What do the clusters and patches of wood suggest to you?

In sculpture we identify both natural and manufactured or man-made shapes. And with shape, because sculpture is three-dimensional, we also pay attention to form, volume, and weight. The three-dimensional shapes in sculpture are called form. In painting, shapes can give an illusion of volume. A square becomes a cube by adding lines or shadows. Form in sculpture has actual volume, a word that describes the density, thickness, and weight of an object or figure. We wonder, "How light or heavy is it?" Or, "What is its size and weight?"

*Pure Drop* by John Chamberlain (FIG. 23) is made from cast-off car parts—hoods, doors, and fenders—crumpled and welded together. The refuse of America's disposable culture is recycled into sculpture. The metal parts fit together like a giant jigsaw puzzle. The tall narrow strip of chrome attached to the bulky "body" pulls the piece off-balance; despite the heaviness of the material the folded shapes appear buoyant, hollow, as if this long-necked, petrified beast is about to take off. The colorful patchwork of shapes on the painted surface adds visual variety. Some sensory words that relate to its imposing form are *tilting, hollow, angular, compact, compressed, vertical*. What does the form remind you of? A giraffe? A prehistoric animal? A meteorite? Or some odd vehicle?

FIG. 23. John Chamberlain, ***Pure Drop***, 1983. Painted and chromium-plated steel, 135" x 72" x 36". Private Collection.

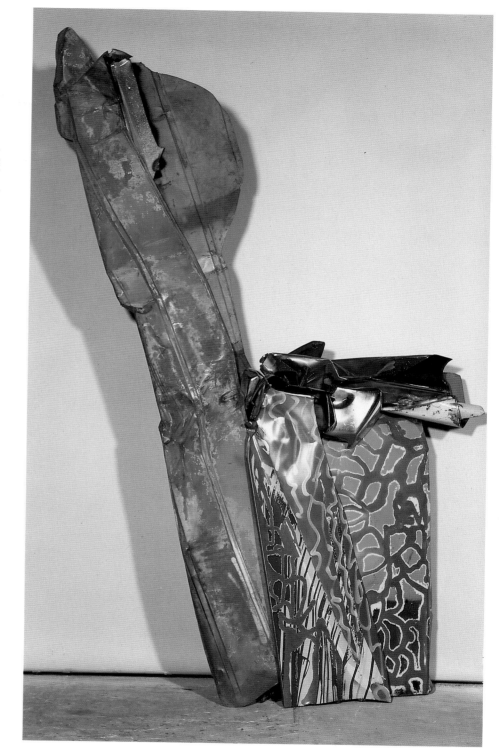

**FIG. 24. Martin Puryear, *Lever No. 3*, 1989. Carved and painted wood, 84½″ x 162″ x 13″.**
National Gallery of Art, Washington, D.C. Gift of the Collectors Committee.

We asked John Chamberlain what in his childhood might have influenced his work. He said:

In Rochester, Indiana, there was a doctor—old Doc Huffman. I remember he had a long beard. A little town always has a token everything. He was the token eccentric. Everyone made fun of him because he collected piles of old stuff—junk. He drove around town in an old 1935 Woody Ford wagon. Very slowly—always keeping it in second gear. I could see his place from my house. Now I think he was pretty brilliant but very eccentric.

Until I was about twelve, I wanted to be an aeronautical engineer. I messed around with airplanes. I had lots of toys with wheels: tricycles, two-wheelers, a dirigible, a zeppelin with wheels, a scooter. Later a kayak. I had all those means of transportation. Now I would assume I wanted to escape.

Shapes and forms can communicate certain feelings because we associate them with similar shapes in real life. For example, free form, meandering, or curved forms are often called biomorphic because they suggest living or natural things.

*Lever No. 3* (FIG. 24) by Martin Puryear, handcrafted out of thin strips of laminated wood, is a biomorphic shape. Tall in height and long, but narrow in width, the form of *Lever No. 3*, unlike *Pure Drop*, does not have much volume. The effect is light, not heavy. Notice its creaturelike qualities: the softly curving humped body, the thrust of the neck curling into a head. Even though we cannot identify it, the form seems familiar, reminding us of a large snail or a small dinosaur.

Some sensory words that come to mind are *matte, curving, striated, smooth, sweeping*. There are no jutting angles, no zigzagging shapes or forms to interfere with the gentle flow of this piece.

Creating the opposite effect are the geometric shapes of Richard Serra's *One-Ton Prop (House of Cards)* (FIG. 25). Four five-hundred-pound plates of lead are propped together, touching only at the corners. The simple flat lead squares are heavy, and they enclose a hollow space. The emptiness at the center of the piece, the rawness of the material, scarred and unpolished lead, and the propped vertical sides of the cube feel impermanent. The title warns us, after all, that this is a *house of cards*, a flimsy structure meant to tumble down at a touch. There is an illusion of danger. The space around it is charged. Serra's art is not tame: it challenges, makes demands, poses risks.

**Richard Serra leaning against a portion of *Twain*, 1976–81, at the Gateway Mall in Saint Louis.**
(Photo © Robert Pettus)

THE SCULPTOR'S EYE

FIG. 25. Richard Serra, *One-Ton Prop (House of Cards)*, 1969. Lead antimony, 4 plates, each 48″ x 48″ x 1″.
The Museum of Modern Art, New York. Gift of the Grinstein Family.

Serra's vision of sculpture, of time arrested, of the power of simple form, relates back to a moment recalled from childhood. He said:

One of my earliest recollections is that of driving with my father, as the sun was coming up, across the Golden Gate Bridge. We were going to the Marine Shipyard, where my father worked as a pipe fitter, to watch the launching of a ship. It was on my birthday in the fall of 1943. I was four. When we arrived, the black, blue, and orange steel-plated tanker was in way, balanced on a perch. It was disproportionately horizontal and to a four-year-old was as large as a skyscraper on its side. I remember walking the arc of the hull with my father, looking at the huge brass propeller, peering through the stays. Then, in a sudden flurry of activity, the shoring props, beams, planks, poles, bars, keep, blocks, all the dunnage, were removed, the cables released, shackles dismantled, the come-alongs unlocked. There was a total incongruity between the displacement of this enormous tonnage and the quickness and agility with which this task was carried out. As the scaffolding was torn apart, the ship moved down the chute toward the sea; there were the accompanying sounds of celebration, screams, foghorns, shouts, whistles. Freed from its stays, the logs rolling, the ship slid off its cradle with an ever-increasing motion. It was a moment of tremendous anxiety as the oiler en route rattled, swayed, tipped, and bounced into the sea, half submerged, to then raise and lift itself and find its balance. Not only had the tanker collected itself, but the witnessing crowd collected itself as the ship went through a transformation from an enormous obdurate weight to a buoyant structure, free, afloat, and adrift. My awe and wonder of that moment remained. All the raw material that I needed is contained in the reserve of this memory, which has become a recurring dream.

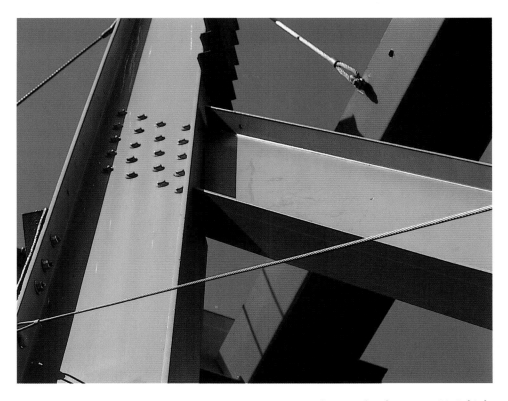

FIG. 26. Mark di Suvero, *Mother Peace*, 1970, DETAIL. **Steel painted red-orange, 39′6″ high.** Storm King Art Center, Mountainville, New York. Gift of the Ralph E. Ogden Foundation.

**Lines.**   We stand in them to go to the movies. We draw them on paper. We learn them for plays. We dare people to cross them. We stay inside them for basketball or tennis. It might therefore be expected that in sculpture the word *line* has several different meanings.

As an axis line, it is an imaginary line we draw through the shapes and forms to indicate direction—the thrust, movement, or dynamics of sculpture.

In *Mother Peace* (FIG. 26) the beams themselves become axis lines. If we were drawing imaginary lines, we would need one for each beam. This is sculpture stripped down, ready for action. The beams are like skeletons, strong bones of sculpture that press into space. Energy made visible.

*Cubic Modular Piece No. 2 (L–Shaped Modular Piece)* (FIG. 27) by Sol Le Witt also is sculpture stripped to its bones, but here the bones are a three-dimensional grid of white lines. These spare, even lines insist on their anonymous repetition, square after square, as regular as if a swarm of mechanical bees had constructed an industrial hive of the future. This grid is a quintessential twentieth-century shape. It could be the structure of a skyscraper, or a gigantic scientific model.

**FIG. 27. Sol Le Witt,** *Cubic Modular Piece No. 2 (L-Shaped Modular Piece),* **1966. Baked enamel on steel, 109⅛″ x 5⅞″ x 59⅞″.** Walker Art Center, Minneapolis. Art Center Acquisition Fund.

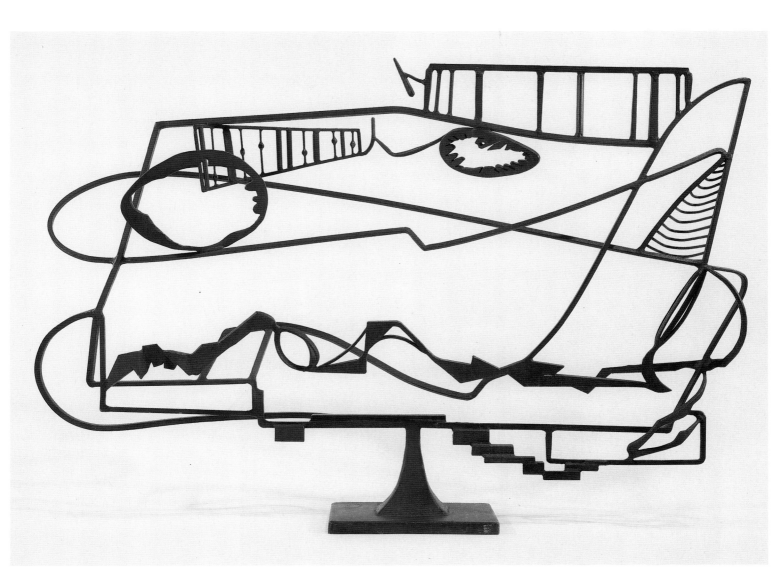

**FIG. 28. David Smith, _Hudson River Landscape_, 1951. Welded steel, 49½" x 75" x 16¾".** Whitney Museum of American Art, New York. Purchase.

The concept of line we take from drawing is the mark a pencil or brush makes on a piece of paper. We picture line as being flat or perhaps as simulating volume. Instead of drawing on the page with pen or paint in _Hudson River Landscape_ (FIG. 28), David Smith has drawn in space.

**David Smith in his studio.**
(Photo © Ugo Mulas)

His line has the swift linear effect of a sketch, but he is working in welded steel, and the line is metal. It exists in three dimensions. The "drawing" is abstract, not realistic, but we can detect railroad tracks that run beside the river, the clouds, and the large broken stones along the banks. Notice the lines and the spaces in between. Are the solid lines or the empty shapes the positive space in this sculpture? There isn't a "right" answer to this question. The interest lies in considering it. The sculptor is experimenting, playing with space and volume. David Smith wrote about his sources of inspiration. In part he said:

> From the way booms sling
> From the ropes and pegs of tent tabernacles
> and side shows at county fairs in Ohio
> from the barefooted memory of unit relationships on locomotives
> sidling
> through Indiana,
> from hopping freights, from putting them together
> and working on their parts in Schenectady
> from everything that happens to circles
> and from the cultured forms of woman and the free growth
> of mountain flowers.

We look at these sculptures, their forms and lines, the way they occupy space, and we remind ourselves again that all works of art are about ideas and feelings. Through talking about the formal elements of each piece and the balance of repetition, size, and scale, we uncover its meaning. We stay in touch with why the work was made, the artist's vision, and our own.

**FIG. 29. Martin Puryear, *Lever #1*, 1988.**
**Red cedar, 167½″ x 132¾″ x 17¾″.**
The Art Institute of Chicago, the A. James Speyer Memorial,
with additional funds provided by UNR Industries in honor of
James W. Alsdorf, Barbara Neff and Solomon Byron Smith Funds.

# 5

# TALKING WITH THE ARTISTS II

## Martin Puryear, Sol Le Witt, Charles Simonds

**M**artin Puryear, Sol Le Witt, and Charles Simonds are all American artists; yet their experiences growing up in America were as different as their art. Puryear handcrafts his pieces out of wood. Le Witt's pristine grids are made in a factory. Charles Simonds builds his villages out of clay. All three challenge our traditional notions about three-dimensional form and the way sculpture occupies space.

FIG. 30. Martin Puryear, *Lever No. 3*, 1989. Carved and painted wood, 84½" x 162" x 13".
National Gallery of Art, Washington, D.C. Gift of the Collectors Committee.

## MARTIN PURYEAR

What does *Lever #1* (FIG. 29) remind you of? A boat? A ladle? A creature? A coffin? Puryear is one of many artists who work in series. Like a song that repeats a melody, each piece is a variation on a theme. Here Martin Puryear talks about *Lever #1* and *Lever No. 3* (FIG. 30), two examples of wooden sculptures from his Lever series.

**Q.** Tell us about these pieces.

**M. P.** The main bodies of the work are solid, made from large pieces of wood glued into a single block and shaped. The curved necks are made from long thin strips glued together in a permanent bend, using a process called lamination. The works belong to a series of sculptures I called *Levers* because each has a main "body," like a neck or a lever. While they are all obviously

**Martin Puryear holding one of the woodworking
tools in his studio.**
(Photo courtesy of the Donald Young Gallery)

man-made constructions or artifacts, what interested me was the way each one also assumed the
character of a "creature." In each work I tried to
make a spirit of the man-made coexist in a single
form with the spirit of a natural, living thing.

**Q.** What was your first experience with art?

**M. P.** I spent my early years in Washington, D.C.
Although my neighborhood was a very poor
area in the 1940s, it was not far from the museums
on Constitution Avenue. In fact we could walk to
the Smithsonian's Museum of Natural History,
which immediately became my favorite. I don't
know which I loved most—looking at the animal
and bird exhibits or visiting the displays of Es-
kimo and American Indian culture. As soon as I
was old enough, I used to go to the museums
alone to sketch the exhibits.

I also visited the National Museum of Art with
my family. I'll never forget my first visit—I must
have been three or four years old. I was struck by
the full-size statues of men and women without
clothes lining the enormous hallways. And I remember the awe I felt when I learned that the
pictures on the walls were actually painted by
hand and not taken with a camera.

**Q.** Did you make art as a child?

**M. P.** From the time I was four or five I persisted in drawing pictures, and my parents encouraged my early efforts. They arranged for me to study with a woman named Cornelia Yuditsky, who gave an art class for children in downtown Washington. She was from Eastern Europe, I believe, and I remember her as a warmhearted person who took your work very seriously. Even though Washington in the 1940s was still rigidly segregated, she welcomed students from all ethnic backgrounds. She had clay for modeling, but I remember at that time all I wanted to do was paint. I'd just come in and get out my colors and find a good easel and go to work. She'd have still lifes set up, but you could paint whatever you wanted. I was especially fascinated by a book of Audubon's bird pictures. When I wasn't painting pictures of birds and wild animals, I was painting Indians. She'd give the gentlest of critiques—just enough to let us know that some things we did were better than others. She would usually give me suggestions about how to solve a problem I'd be struggling with, but one day she said, "This is not so good. We all have bad days sometimes." I

got the idea very early that although it was fun to do art, there existed values beyond the pleasure of making the work.

**Q.** Wood is one of your favorite materials. Did you learn woodworking as a child?

**M. P.** When I was young, I began to work with wood in my father's workshop. Later, while I was in college, I built some musical instruments and furniture with the help of books. At first the making of these things was very separate from my interest in art, but at a certain point they came together. After college I went to teach in the Sierra Leone, on the west coast of Africa, and there I met craftsmen who worked in traditional ways making woodwork, pottery, and textiles. I spent a lot of time with the woodworkers. They considered themselves simply carpenters, but they were enormously versatile. They made furniture and wooden truck bodies, caskets for burying the dead, or entire houses, all totally by hand with no machinery.

After Africa, I went to Sweden to study art, and it was there that I began to concentrate on making sculpture, and to work using methods of construction instead of carving or modeling.

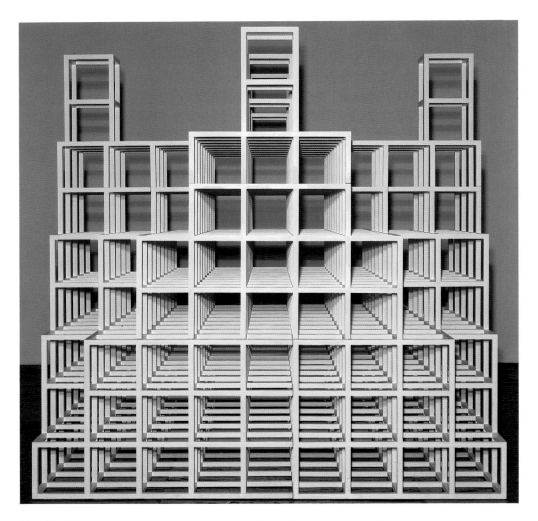

FIG. 31. Sol Le Witt, *Five Towers*, 1986. Painted wood, 8 units, overall: 86⁹⁄₁₆″ x 86⁹⁄₁₆″ x 86⁹⁄₁₆″.
Whitney Museum of American Art, New York. Purchase with funds from the Louis and Bessie Adler Foundation, Inc.
(Seymour M. Klein, President), the John I. H. Baur Purchase Fund, the Grace Belt Endowed Purchase Fund, the Sondra
and Charles Gilman, Jr., Foundation, Inc., the List Purchase Fund, and the Painting and Sculpture Committee.

## SOL LE WITT

"What you see is what you get" is an expression often associated with the minimalist sculptures of Sol Le Witt. In other words, his pieces are not intended to symbolize or represent anything other than themselves. His *Five Towers* (FIG. 31) and *Cubic Modular Piece No. 2* (*L–Shaped Modular Piece*) (FIG. 32) contain at least two important pre-occupations of twentieth-century artists. They are based on a grid structure, like most of our skyscrapers, and they are fabricated, like most of our possessions, at a manufacturer, according to the artist's directions. Once you peer inside those squares within squares that seem to recede into infinity, you realize simplicity of form does not necessarily mean simplicity of experience.

**Q.** Is there a mathematical basis to your work?

**S. L.** My work isn't based on a particular mathematical system. I had the usual math and plane geometry at school; nothing more. It's more an innate sensibility, a sense of order rather than actual knowledge.

**Q.** You had these pieces manufactured, didn't you? Why did you choose to make them white?

**S. L.** The three-dimensional objects were made at the fabricators. To use color would have been unnecessary. White was easiest in terms of the three-dimensional grids being read or understood. These objects are based on human scale. My own size.

**Q.** What was the first experience with art that you remember?

**S. L.** When I was very young, either in second or third grade, I remember doing a long drawing of a bus. We lived above my aunt's grocery store, so I used big sheets of white wrapping paper. Now my children use the materials in my studio. One likes to build with three dimensions, cardboard shoe boxes, and things; the other draws on a flat surface. I want my work to appeal to all the senses, but I also want it to be understood. It involves thinking; it's not about taking a bath.

**Q.** Did you make art as a child?

**S. L.** I always drew. My parents were very supportive. My father was a doctor, my mother a

**FIG. 32. Sol Le Witt, *Cubic Modular Piece No. 2 (L-Shaped Modular Piece)*, 1966. Baked enamel on steel, 109⅛" x 5⅞" x 59⅞".**
Walker Art Center, Minneapolis, Art Center Acquisition Fund.

nurse. She used to take me to art classes at the Wadsworth Atheneum. Later I went to the School of Fine Arts at Syracuse University. When I moved to New York, I supported myself as a graphic designer. I worked for an architect and *Seventeen Magazine*. I still like to do graphics. It's fun work for me.

FIG. 33. Charles Simonds, *Dwellings*, 1981, DETAIL (one of eight photographs). Unfired clay wall relief, 96" x 528". Museum of Contemporary Art, Chicago. Gift of Douglas and Carol Cohen.

## CHARLES SIMONDS

When we encounter Charles Simonds's miniature clay villages, we feel like Gulliver visiting the Lilliputians. This is an installation piece—the artist designed it for a particular space and built (or installed) it there. It is a permanent installation, but many of the clay villages Charles Simonds has been building for the last fifteen years are temporary installations, constructed in abandoned buildings and vacant lots. Some are small, others are more elaborate. While the artist is working, passersby stop, give advice, get involved. These buildings may last an hour or a week before they are destroyed. No one attempts to preserve them, although sometimes photographs are taken to serve as a record. Their existence is as fleeting as a sand castle.

**Q.** Why do you often choose to make art that will disappear?

**C. S.** For me, the pleasure and necessity of these works is in the making of them: the dramatic effect for people of seeing something come to be carefully, slowly before their eyes. That is the important experience. The destruction is comparatively much less important. The buildings are only artifacts of the experience.

**Q.** How are the permanent pieces such as *Dwellings, 1981* (FIG. 33) different from the temporary installations?

**C. S.** The permanent works are bigger and more elaborate than the temporary pieces; they are built more carefully—*Dwellings* took about seventeen days. There weren't any spectators when I built it. And the sense of time isn't the same. The time within the buildings is a long, deep time, whereas the time of the viewers is a fleeting time. You look for a moment and then you move on.

**Q.** Why do you work in this size?

**C. S.** I work small as a kind of economy of time and energy. Also as a way of infesting a neighborhood with my villages. Some of the work is small, some is now large. One in Korea is full-size. The pieces themselves are scaleless. Once you are in the dwelling, it is full-scale. There is no distortion. The proportions are human, but smaller.

**Q.** We are reminded of abandoned cliff dwellings of the Native American Pueblo Indians. Did you have that in mind when you began?

**C. S.** My mother thinks I was influenced by a childhood trip, but I'm not convinced. Americans cast these dwellings in the Southwest, but if I work in Paris, then people think they come from Morocco or North Africa, and in Spain they think the buildings are Spanish. The commonality in all cultures is a primitive dwelling place.

**Q.** How did you begin working with clay?

**C. S.** I knew very early that it was what I was going to do with my life. I was in high school. My brother had gone off to college and left behind some Plasticine, some clay. One night I took some of it and made a sculpture of a lying-down wrestler, with all the musculature. I remember the sensation of working with the clay was overwhelming. The feeling of the clay, the sense of connectedness, that my hands could do this thing, was stunning. I took the wrestler to school in a shoe box, but no one believed me—no one believed I had made it. I had never done anything like it before, never shown any talent or interest in this area. So the next day I took some clay to school and in front of everyone I made another figure. Before that everyone assumed I would be a mathematician. But after I made the

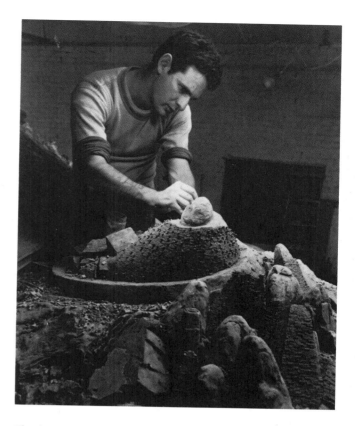

**Charles Simonds working on one of his small-scale pieces.** (Photo © Daniel Heald. Courtesy of the Leo Castelli Gallery)

first sculpture, I knew what I was going to do, seriously, with my life.

After that I studied with two sculptors who lived in Greenwich Village. They mostly made angels for churches and things. Many of the gestures I learned then, I use now. Ways of handling the clay and how it feels in my hands, I relate them back to those first experiences.

After college at Berkeley, I went to Rutgers, in New Jersey, to graduate school. There were some clay pits near the school and I went out and dug the clay for my work. I feel that connection between us—the body, the house, and the earth.

**FIG. 34. Robert Rauschenberg, *Monogram*, 1955–59. Stuffed goat, tire, mixed media, and canvas, 64″ x 63″ x 37″.**
Statens Konstmuseer, Stockholm, Sweden.

# 6

# WHAT IS IT MADE OF?

The goat, dignified in spite of the tire around his stomach, stands in the center of *Monogram* (FIG. 34) by Robert Rauschenberg. He is so incongruously satisfying that we can't help smiling. What is he doing in an art museum? We fantasize he, too, wonders at his surroundings. We can be sure that Rauschenberg didn't decide "What *Monogram* needs is a stuffed goat," and set out to find one. He saw it in a store window one day, liked the way it looked, and decided to bring it home. Later he used it in *Monogram*. The goat has the air of an inspiration.

Think of a place where you keep mementos. A stone picked up on the beach, a well-loved doll or model plane, a program from a rock concert— these items, selected and arranged together, become your assemblage and tell something about your life and point of view. Rauschenberg said, "I want to work in the gap between art and life." What is he saying in this gap with his goat? There are no boundaries. Everything is included.

You can make art out of anything: a stuffed animal, Coke bottles, clay from a New Jersey clay pit, your old overcoat, marble, bronze, wood, stainless steel, piles of earth, smashed tin cans, plaster, fiberglass, latex, automobile fenders, newspaper clippings and outdated magazines, paper, plastic, glass, grass, dirty sneakers, new gloves, broken chairs, odd lengths of chain, house paint, bolts, doorknobs, hair, canvas, granite, lead, chicken bones, shovels and . . . the list goes on.

Each artist makes his or her own choice of these materials. Louise Bourgeois, an artist who employs many different substances including wood, plaster, found objects, stone, and marble, said:

I always want to make the work better. So when I have made it in plaster, I am not satisfied with that. And I say, "If I made it in stone, I would have a better chance to communicate what I want to say." So I will go from one material to another.

**Louise Bourgeois at work in her studio.**
(Photo © Claudio Edinger. Courtesy of the Robert Miller Gallery)

But the material to me is a means, not an end. I am not saying to you, "Look at this beautiful stone." The stone is only what you make of it. The end is what you say. I want affirmation. I want to say what I mean.

The material from which an artwork is made has texture, color, and a surface that absorbs or reflects light. These become the tools or means to the expressive qualities of the sculpture.

**Texture.**  The refined curves of carved marble, the rusty battered surface of cast-off metal, or the cool, glossy finish of a ceramic piece, each carries its own sensation. Touching a sculpture, like moving around it, activates our experience of it. Unless the material itself has sharp or jagged edges and warns us away, only a "DON'T TOUCH" sign prevents us from responding to this urge. Luckily, we perceive texture with our eyes as well as our hands.

*Décontractée* (FIG. 35) by Louise Bourgeois is carved from one block of marble. The soft polished luster of the delicate, open hands and slim forearms is in contrast to the rough texture of the base. Contrasts give a sculpture variety and interest. We know the hands are stone hard, yet the surface has the silky sheen of pale, resilient flesh. Sculptors are attracted to marble because it can suggest skin tone. The lines of the palms are so faithfully reproduced that a fortune-teller

**FIG. 35. Louise Bourgeois, *Décontractée*, 1990. Pink marble & steel, 28½" x 36" x 23" overall.**

could read the future in them. The arms are long and slender, the veins clearly visible. In their graceful symmetry *Décontractée* reminds us of a fragment from an ancient statue. The piece is ceremonial in feeling. Bourgeois has chiseled cuts and marks in a repeated pattern, which give the surface of the base a textural rhythm. The base could be an altar, the hands a sacrifice.

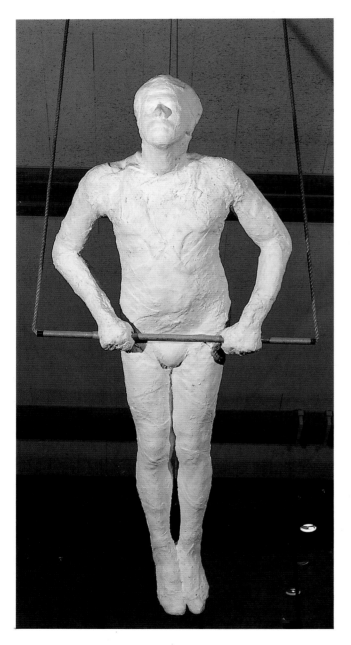

**FIG. 36. George Segal, *Trapeze*, 1971. Plaster, rope, metal, and wood, 72" x 36". Wadsworth Atheneum, Hartford. Gift of Joseph L. Schulman and an anonymous donor.**

The texture of *Décontractée* simulates skin tone; the texture of *Trapeze* (FIG. 36) flaunts its materials. Plaster—plain, lumpy, bumpy, coarse, and rough. The artist doesn't make any attempt to fool us by smoothing or painting. We can see the edges of the bandages, the weave and imprint of the fabric, the way in which it was wrapped around the model. The raw surface still bears the marks of its making. We are aware that hidden inside the cast is the mold of a real person, and this gives the piece its haunting presence.

The ragged, battered *Horse* (FIG. 37) by Deborah Butterfield stands, life-size, head down, her hide layers of pitted metal. Thin straps crisscross the body and hang from the neck suggesting the remnants of bridle and tack, emblems of a life of hard labor. The old, rough-textured metal gives the horse a history, not only as in the trapeze artist, of its making, but also a narrative history—this is a horse with a past. Some words that come to mind are *victim/survivor*, *work/rest*, *tough/vulnerable*. These words in turn point to the deeper meaning of the work. We don't see it as a portrait of a real horse or an idealized horse, but as a symbol for someone or something that has come through hard times.

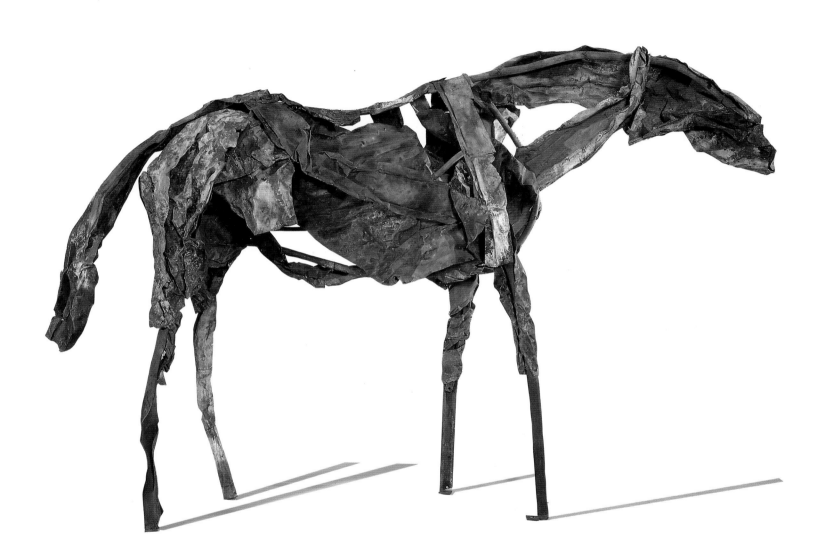

**FIG. 37. Deborah Butterfield, *Horse*, 1985. Construction of painted and rusted sheet steel, wire and steel tubing, 82⅛″ x 118⅝″ x 34¼″.**
Hirshhorn Museum and Sculpture Garden, Smithsonian Institution, Washington, D.C. The Thomas M. Evans, Jerome L. Green, Joseph H. Hirshhorn, and Sydney and Frances Lewis Purchase Fund.

**Color.** What does color do? It appeals to our senses, it delights our eye, and it affects our emotions. Almost automatically, we identify hot colors and cool ones, exciting colors and peaceful ones.

Sometimes artists work with material in its natural state, but this doesn't mean it is colorless. Stones range in color. Marble is quarried in shades from pure white to rose, black, and even deep green. Wood varies from the black of ebony to the pale blond of ash. Bronze can be burnished to a brassy sheen, patinated in a greenish blue or rubbed in a mixture of dark and gleaming patinas like the surface of *Untitled, 1984* (FIG. 38 detail). Joel Shapiro told us he makes wood models and then casts them in lead or bronze. Up close you can see the texture of

the wood preserved in the metal cast, complete with notches and the striated pattern of the wood grain. The color of the patina shading from rust to brown-gray also alludes back to the color of the wood. Once more we make a connection to the hand of the artist. The struggle of this falling figure, Shapiro implies, is not only in the piece but in me and in you.

Sometimes sculpture is painted. Using twentieth-century materials such as steel and plastic, artists gained a new attitude toward color. Alexander Calder, who painted his steel stabiles and mobiles, said, "You have to paint the steel anyway to protect it, so why paint it gray, why not paint it red?"

In Calder's *Indian Feathers* (FIG. 39) five flat shapes, abstract but recognizable as feathers,

FIG. 38. Joel Shapiro, *Untitled, 1984,* DETAIL. Bronze, 79¼" x 78¼" x 38¾". St. Louis Art Museum. Gift of Mr. and Mrs. Barney A. Ebsworth.

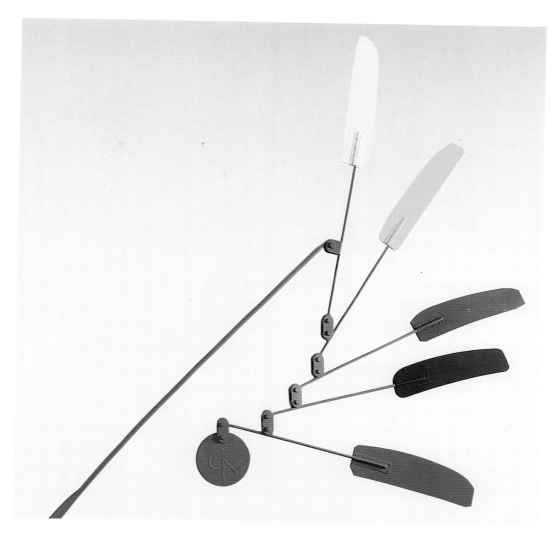

FIG. 39. Alexander Calder, *Indian Feathers*, 1969. Painted aluminum sheet and stainless steel rods, 136¾" x 91" x 63". Whitney Museum of American Art, New York. Purchase with funds from the Howard and Jean Lipman Foundation, Inc.

hang from a long red supporting pole anchored to the ground by a large red circle of steel. What you can't tell from the photograph is that this is a moving sculpture, called a mobile. Thin wires are connected in such a way that any slight current of air will cause the shapes to move. Areas of flat primary color—red, yellow, and blue as well as black and white—enhance the biomorphic shapes. This is not a realistic representation of a First American war bonnet, but in its bright, free swinging movement we can imagine a warrior riding along with the wind gently blowing the feathers of his headdress.

Colors, like shapes, have their own associations. Would *Indian Feathers* be different if we switched the color? Suppose it had been painted gray or left unpainted, steel colored, perhaps rusted and weathered? We can imagine it heavier and more serious. The color lightens the metal shapes to suit their airy movements.

In keeping with the question "What do we see?", the artist Nancy Graves describes this outdoor sculpture (FIG. 40).

The title *Harvester K.C.* (or Kansas City), like the elements in the eighteen-foot-tall sculpture, are particular to the Midwest. A triangular canopy of cast-bronze leaves—maple and bloodroot—is supported by stainless-steel-cut elements representing lakes and streams. On two sides of the canopy are eighteen-inch-tall bronze ears of corn and wheat which span the diamond-shaped directly cast rope. Projecting through the canopy are two vertical elements: a sickle bar twice scale and a river or winged form.

Spanning at mid-height and supporting the sickle bar and river is a triangular fence made of acetylene-torch-cut stainless steel which visually bisects the sides of the triangular leaf canopy. A cultivator rests atop one of the points of the triangle. A windmill and eighteen-inch-diameter sunflowers welded to the three-inch stainless steel armature comprise the basic elements.

Nancy Graves hand paints her sculptures, but in contrast to the flat, primary colors of Calder, she uses glossy paint in a loose brushy way. In *Harvester K.C.* many of the shapes are cast from actual plants, but they are not painted to look authentic. The whole construction rises and twines with an air of delicate authority, balanced on a base of brightly colored sunflowers that seem too fragile to support such a towering structure. Some sensory words that describe the color are *bright, acidic, harsh,* and *shiny.*

Nancy Graves said:

Nature has always held a special intensity for me. The Berkshire Museum [in Massachusetts, where she grew up] was typical of small American city institutions. A sculpture and painting survey of Western art was displayed on one floor and natural history on the other. My father, who was on the museum staff, introduced me to the preparators behind the scenes. I visibly remember our visits to Jonas Brothers, the creators of dioramas and taxidermy habitats. So early on I made a mental and visual link between the final display and illusionary methods and techniques of its making. Later the process of transformation became integral to my own art from the first sculpture, the camels, to the present where process or the making of the work is exposed and art and the natural sciences are merged.

FIG. 40. Nancy Graves,
*Harvester K.C.*, 1986.
Stainless steel and bronze
with polyurethane paint,
18′ x 8′ x 14′.
Courtesy of United Missouri Bank
Collection, Kansas City, Missouri.

FIG. 41. Isamu Noguchi, *Core*
*(Cored Sculpture)*, 1978. Basalt, 74".
Isamu Noguchi Garden Museum, Long Island City, New York.

**Light.** When we discuss texture and color in sculpture, we are also talking about light. Sculptors have always known that the way light falls on a sculpture and the shadows cast by its shapes and forms become part of the effect of the sculpture. For example, on a smooth surface the light reflects evenly. On a rough surface the reflections are uneven.

*Core* (FIG. 41) by Isamu Noguchi, a six-foot-tall monolithic sculpture, stands outside in a courtyard garden. The appearance of *Core* is affected by weather—cloudy or sunny—and light at different times of day. The mood of the piece changes as the sun casts flickering light and shadows on its rough surface. From one view the natural stone has rusted edges, a coarse-grained texture, oxidized in earth tones of orange and pale sandy-gray. Two holes have been drilled into the basalt—down the center from the top and through the side—allowing the light to enter the stone. There is a feeling of serenity and also of strength. Noguchi releases the possibilities inherent in the material. We are reminded of a doorway, a boulder, a standing stone carrying memories of Japanese sculpture gardens, of Stonehenge. The artist said to a visitor to his studio, "Go ahead. Put your head into it. Then you will know what the inside of a stone feels like."

Three stainless steel rectangles lie stacked against a steel triangular shape. In contrast to *Core*, the sleek surface of Beverly Pepper's *Fallen*

THE SCULPTOR'S EYE

**FIG. 42. Beverly Pepper, *Fallen Sky*, 1968. Stainless steel and baked enamel, 105″ x 181″ x 58″.**
Hirshhorn Museum and Sculpture Garden, Smithsonian Institution, Washington, D.C.

*Sky* (FIG. 42) reflects light, as well as the negative space around the triangles—sky, the grass, even the viewer become an ever-changing part of the composition. Only the painted blue outside planes remain constant. These reflections transform the space, make it ambiguous, so that the shifting negative space becomes part of the composition. Some words that come to mind are *industrial, machine, manufacturing, power, strength, mirror.*

In *Untitled* (FIG. 43) by Dan Flavin the material itself is a light source. The various colors in the bright fluorescent tubes blend where they meet and fill the room with a red glow that has shadows of purple, magenta, and strange gray-green. The walls, the floor, the viewer are all bathed in a radiant light. If you stand beside it, your face will be one color, your hands another. You become a part of the work.

*Untitled* appears to be a pure grid with no references to any known object other than perhaps strip lighting, but the artist's use of the neon colors triggers certain cultural references. What associations do we make to the fluorescent tubes and bright colors? Video games. Arcades. Advertising signs and slogans. Dan Flavin has painted with light, and indeed, like *Monogram*, this piece stands somewhere between sculpture and painting. This is sculpture with a beat, with the almost invisible pulse and buzz of fluorescent lights.

If you were creating a dance inspired by Dan Flavin's *Untitled*, what would it be like? What kind of music would you choose?

By exploring other art forms—music, dance, or poetry—we find out more about responses to the visual arts. If we give free rein to our own imaginations, we can bypass the part of us that says, "Hmmmm. It seems to me to be possible that . . ." and get in touch with the part of us that says, "Oh, wow . . . I feel . . . I love it."

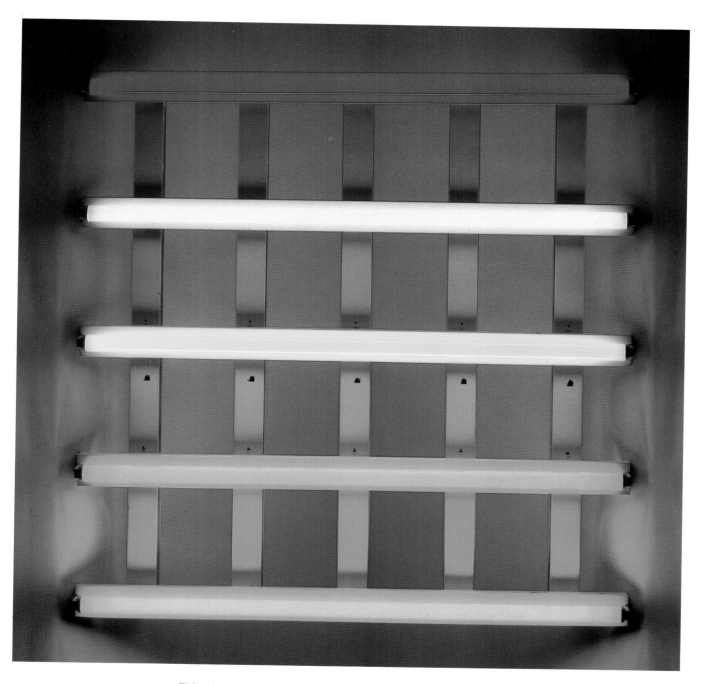

**FIG. 43. Dan Flavin, *Untitled*, 1987. Fluorescent light, 48″ x 48″.**
Greenberg Gallery, St. Louis.

# 7

# TALKING WITH THE ARTISTS III

**Joel Shapiro, Deborah Butterfield,
Beverly Pepper, Claes Oldenburg**

The monumental abstract forms of Beverly Pepper. The dynamic figures and cast-metal houses of Joel Shapiro. The poetic scrap-metal horses of Deborah Butterfield. The towering baseball bat of Claes Oldenburg. What do these works have in common? Like many contemporary American sculptures, all of them are open forms made of welded metal.

## JOEL SHAPIRO

Many of Joel Shapiro's works are small-scale and figurative, but they also function as abstract forms. His inspiration comes from memories and images of his past.

The small house of *House on a Field* (FIG. 44) was made from wood and set on a clay field; then the model was cast in lead. Once a mold is made, it usually is possible to cast more than one piece. *House on a Field* is one of three pieces cast from the same mold. The wooden frame is an integral part of the piece. The artist wanted the contrast of wood and lead.

**FIG. 44. Joel Shapiro, *House on a Field*, 1975–77. 21″ x 21¾″ x 28¾″ x 2″. Bronze with a wooden base.** Private Collection.

**Q.** Where did you get your idea for *House on a Field*?

**J. S.** The houses are all about putting one's past in order, a process of evolution. They utilize memory and refer back to ideal states or remembered states. I was immersed in making sculpture and wanted to find images that were necessary to me. It had to do with necessity, finding images that were internal without abandoning a belief in modernism. I didn't want the gloppy surfaces of abstract expressionism; nor did I want them to be minimalist in that they referred only to the

**Behind Joel Shapiro, on the desk, you can see small working models—called maquettes—of some of his sculptures.**
(Photo © Douglas Rice. Courtesy of Paula Cooper Gallery)

external. The pieces are about a mental state, and I wanted to develop my own meaningful vocabulary.

**Q.** Why are your houses so small?

**J. S.** I didn't intend them to be miniaturized. That just seemed appropriate. They have a formal concern but deal in intimate subject matter.

**Q.** Why did you cast them?

**J. S.** I wanted to insist on them. First I carved them out of wood. The image appears out of the block of wood. By casting them in lead they retain the memory, insist on it. They make the statement emphatic and tender at the same time. They have an aggressive external form, but the subject, the house, is internal. I pare down the form and load up the content.

**Q.** What was your first encounter with art?

**J. S.** I was exposed to art at an early age. My father was a physician, my mother a scientist. My father had patients who were artists, and so we had contemporary works in the house. They were interested in modern art and always believed in it, believed in museums as a cultural entity. So I grew up going to museums with them and enjoyed the experience. When I was about five or six, my mother organized art classes in the basement of our house. The teacher was a serious artist from Germany. I remember we painted and did ceramics. Growing up, I took classes at school and at the Museum of Modern Art. I drew all the time. It was the one thing I was really good at. I had the feeling that my work was good and I enjoyed the process. But teachers recognized it as well. It never occurred to me that I could be an artist. My parents knew artists who were always struggling. So I didn't pursue it until my last year of college. I was expected to be a doctor and it took a long time to sort that out. Artists have to sacrifice traditional values. It's difficult to be in the world and pursue your work.

## DEBORAH BUTTERFIELD

We began the section on materials by observing that sculpture can be fashioned from anything. This artist uses found material, old metal that she pounds, welds, and clamps into new shapes to make her pieces. The material, worn and burnished, gives Butterfield's subject, studies of horses, a poignant beauty and sense of history.

**Deborah Butterfield at work.**
(Photo © R. Milon.
Courtesy of Deborah Butterfield)

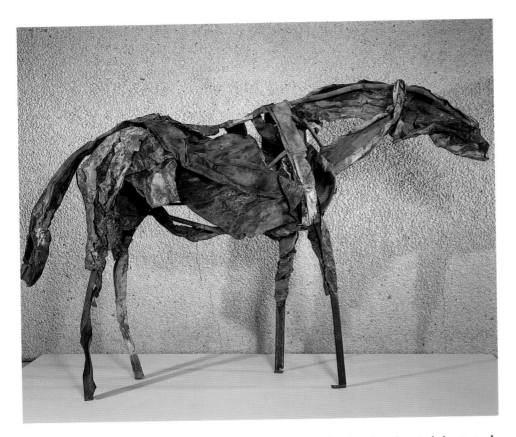

FIG. 45. Deborah Butterfield, *Horse*, 1985. Construction of painted and rusted sheet steel, wire and steel tubing, 82⅛" x 118⅝" x 34¼". Hirshhorn Museum and Sculpture Garden, Smithsonian Institution, Washington, D.C. The Thomas M. Evans, Jerome L. Green, Joseph H. Hirshhorn, and Sydney and Frances Lewis Purchase Fund.

**Q.** What does the horse symbolize for you?

**D. B.** I never see the horse as a victim. They look tough. They have a kind of pathos, but I don't intentionally make them sad. I try to let the feeling of the material's previous life come through. The Hirshhorn piece, *Horse* (FIG. 45), was made out of the galvanized steel from a burned-down pea cannery. Although the material had a rough life and I tried to preserve that, the power of the horse comes through. In a sense it's a metaphor for life. The materials of our bodies get beaten up over time, but our spirits get stronger. I made that piece right after my first child, Wilder, was born. I was worried I could never make art again, the experience of having a child was so strong, but when I went back to my studio, I was filled with power and made that piece myself without an assistant. My pieces are really self-portraits, subjective. By using the horse as my subject matter rather than a human form, I can step in and out of it. The viewer can do the same.

**Q.** How are your pieces constructed?

**D. B.** I rely on forms that I find, but generally I don't rely on heavy equipment. I use materials that I can clamp, bend, and pound with a sledgehammer myself. Sometimes I stand and stomp on it. Or I use several people to pull and bend it. I weld the pieces of metal together, then go back over it with acid to undo the damage done by welding. Acid on hot steel turns it back to its original rusted finish. I believe in poetic license. To make the work cohesive, I'll do whatever I need to do. When the piece goes out of the studio, it takes on a life of its own. But I want it to be as strong as it can be.

**Q.** When did you become fascinated with horses?

**D. B.** I was born on the day of the Kentucky Derby. Perhaps that's part of the problem. But once I saw a horse for the first time, that was it. In the early fifties my father used to take me to Peacock Ranch. It was a western Gene Autry kind of place that had pony rides and a merry-go-round. I headed straight for the real ponies. I enjoyed riding horses, being around them, drawing them. I always drew as a child. The San Diego Zoo and the Art Museum offered classes in drawing the animals at the zoo. I was around nine or ten. We actually went into the snake house or sat among the tortoises, played with lion cubs, and drew in the freezing penguin house.

I loved spending time with a friend of my parents who was a horse doctor. He was my mentor. I often stayed at his ranch on weekends and helped. I remember one Christmas sitting and holding a horse dying from lockjaw. A tetanus shot only cost a dollar, but the people hadn't bothered. Here was this man spending Christmas trying to save a dying animal while the horse's owners were at home celebrating the holiday. I was always torn between wanting to be an artist or a veterinarian. That's how I ended up at U.C. Davis—a good art school and a good vet school.

**Q.** What was your first experience with art?

**D. B.** I started as a potter and later did ceramic saddles because I was afraid to do horses. In a way the saddle was the closest state between the person and the horse. Eventually I started doing what I wanted to do. It took courage. I was teased in art school for doing life-size plaster horses. Everyone else was doing conceptual art; mine was intensely personal but seemed pretty academic until I painted horses.

## BEVERLY PEPPER

At first it may be difficult to figure out the relationship between *Fallen Sky* (FIG. 46), a welded metal piece, and *Cromlech Glen* (FIG. 47) a huge earthwork that rises up in a clearing in the woods like an ancient Mayan monument or a First American mound. But as the artist tells us, intuitions about the solid versus the void (another way of talking about positive and negative space) that she began to investigate in early works such as *Fallen Sky* led to later works like *Cromlech Glen*.

**Q.** What was your concept for *Fallen Sky*? And how did your work evolve from that?
**B. P.** The stainless steel works of the sixties were concerned with the solid versus the void, the spaces in between, and the way the work changes as you move around it. In these early stainless pieces, the ones with highly reflective surfaces, open squares with mirrored sides, I became aware of the importance of the reflections creating surface illusion within the work. The reflected grass surrounding a work became a part of the work. I was "using" the grass. So I tried using real grass in my work.

**FIG. 46. Beverly Pepper, *Fallen Sky*, 1968.**
**Stainless steel and baked enamel, 105″ x 181″ x 58″.**
Hirshhorn Museum and Sculpture Garden, Smithsonian Institution, Washington, D.C.

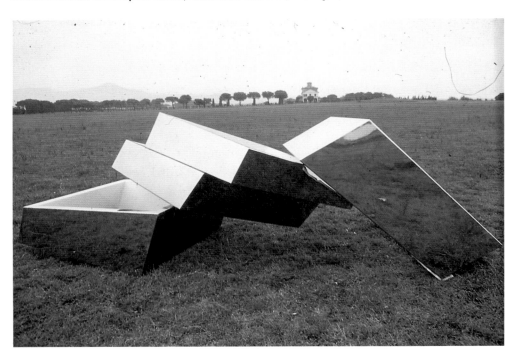

FIG. 47. Beverly Pepper, *Cromlech Glen*, 1985–90. Rock, earth, evergreen trees, sod, and flagstones, 25′ x 130′ x 90′. Laumeier Sculpture Park, St. Louis.

The reflections in *Fallen Sky* are an important part of the effect, but the sculpture could be moved to another location. Only what was reflected would alter. *Cromlech Glen* cannot be moved. It was built to fit into that particular place, making it—like most earthworks—specific to its site.

**Q.** You appear to be working more and more on commissions for public places.

**B. P.** I am essentially a studio artist. I approach public commissions with the same attitude I have in my studio. I like the problems. Problems make me stretch. When given a defined space, you start with a kind of frame that has to be broken. It happens that the scale of my works is very monumental. The works adapt themselves very well to public places. You can't teach anyone scale. Some artists take small things and make them big. I think the proportions of my small things are big. It has nothing to do with size. It has to do with

**Beverly Pepper, welder's mask in place,
working on one of her sculptures.**
(Photo © Dan Budnik. Courtesy of Beverly Pepper)

a feeling of monumentality. A sense of scale is probably a natural talent. It's very difficult to teach.

I also am drawn to open spaces. One of the reasons I live in Todi [a small Italian town] or seek out Santa Fe is that wonderful sky. Why am I so in love with huge spaces—the beautiful sky? Under those skies we become less important. Native Americans have always understood that in such vastness, in such endless mystery, how can man feel so important? It's a complicated concept and I try frequently to enter into that timelessness . . . to try to reflect it.

**Q.** As a child in Brooklyn, were you interested in making art?

**B. P.** I didn't decide to be an artist. I *was* an artist, always drawing. I can't remember not being an artist. But I kept wanting to be a "real" artist. When I was twelve I won a scholarship and took Saturday classes at Pratt. Even before I was in school, I did all my older brother's and sister's drawings, all their geography maps, et cetera. Later when I got their teachers, they didn't believe I was doing my own work. "Let me draw," I remember saying. "I can draw anything you want me to."

I could draw anything, but drawing doesn't make you an artist . . . art is in your head. It's how you think, and what you think. Artists work to complete themselves. The art completes whatever is missing, whatever isn't there. No matter what else is going on, I only feel right when I'm working.

FIG. 48. Claes Oldenburg, *Floor Cone (Giant Ice-Cream Cone)*, 1962. Synthetic polymer paint on canvas filled with foam rubber and cardboard boxes, 53¾" x 11'4" x 56". The Museum of Modern Art, New York. Gift of Philip Johnson.

## CLAES OLDENBURG

Pop artist Claes Oldenburg takes our expectations about an object and turns them upside down and inside out. Small becomes large. Hard becomes soft. Solid becomes transparent. Along the way, objects are metamorphasized, transformed into something new.

**Q.** Is there an element of chance in the way *Floor Cone* (FIG. 48) falls on the floor or do you give directions for the installation?

**C. O.** There is a limit to what it can do because of the seams in the construction. So the way it is arranged is chance but within limits. Chance, the situation, and also the action of time on the fabric. It tends to settle. It was first installed lying down in the Green Gallery in 1962 and then propped up against the wall in the Dwan Gallery in L.A. in 1963. Dennis Hopper, who later became an actor, was taking photographs then. We rented a trailer and drove the cone around. We took pictures of it in crazy positions—for example, lying on the runway of the Santa Monica Airport.

**Q.** What's inside of it?

**C. O.** *Floor Cone* is stuffed with hard and soft

**Claes Oldenburg and Coosje van Bruggen.**
(Photo © Robert Mapplethorpe 1986. Courtesy of The Pace Gallery.)

material. The soft material is foam rubber cut up in chunks. The hard material is empty ice cream cartons. The cartons hold the shape. I wanted the soft sculpture to be like the human body that has hard and soft elements inside of it.

**Q.** How did you begin to make monuments?

**C. O.** *Batcolumn* in 1977 was the first sculpture made for a particular city. There were several subjects considered before a bat. A fireplug was one possibility and a spoon on its end (with the bowl stuck in the ground). The handle of the spoon had a profile like a bat. I wanted a vertical shape to echo the verticality of Chicago. One is very aware of the vertical in Chicago because it is on flat land. The skyline of Chicago is like tombstones coming up out of the lake. It's a good city for architecture. *Batcolumn* is a kind of homage to the steel structures of Chicago. There is also a relationship to certain columns in a train station that existed near the site, which has since been torn down. At the time *Batcolumn* went up, there wasn't anything much in the area. It was part of Skid Row. Now it's surrounded by tall buildings.

**Q.** When did you and Coosje [his wife, artist Coosje van Bruggen] start working together?

**C. O.** This was one of the first pieces Coosje and I worked on together. Coosje came into it after its construction and suggested gray for the color. We mixed a particular kind of gray together.

*Batcolumn* was conceived as a simple, well-known object one would touch, lay hands on, made large. Besides the scale transformation, the object is also opened up, made transparent. I think of it as a rising balloon. It is deliberately related to certain architecture, the John Hancock Building (in Chicago), the Loop elevated train supports, the water towers on roofs, for example. Coosje and I try to relate our sculptures to the site, and we suggest in a low-key way that they could be emblems for the city. They are a combination of our personal fantasy and what we observe in a place.

**Q.** You grew up in Chicago, didn't you?

**C. O.** I was born in Sweden and after some years in Norway came to Chicago at the age of seven. I lived there for twenty-one years. I had a certain talent for drawing but at first I didn't connect it to a career. After I got out of college I went back to Chicago, where I worked for a year and a half as an apprentice newspaper reporter before finally deciding to study art.

**Q.** Art is a natural language for children. . . .

**C. O.** Yes, unfortunately most people give it up. I was visual from the beginning but it was probably encouraged by the fact that when I came to Chicago I couldn't speak a word of English. When you can't speak the verbal language you have to depend on your vision and on representing things—the language of seeing.

I have an active imagination. I developed a private world, an imaginary country I called Neubern, which was part Swedish, part American. I made several books and newspapers about this country, drawing maps, making charts, and illustrating things like fire engines. Later in adolescence I made model airplanes, sometimes changing the design so they looked more the way I wanted them to.

I started as a painter but after a while I didn't like the flatness. I wanted to touch the object. So I combine mass and color: I shape a subject and then I paint it.

I believe the art, when it's made, should be direct and instinctual, though another side of me is intellectual and I enjoy trying to analyze my impulses. Also I like to lay an intellectual groundwork for instinctive behavior.

# 8

# THE "WOW" EXPERIENCE

A dazzling flash of lightning against the dark sky. A silvery waterfall cascading down a rocky cliff. A colorful mobile bending and turning in the wind. Visual images are all around us. Their textures and patterns, their rhythms and variety, add richness to our lives. What sets art apart is that it is created by human beings—by us and for us—to convey our deepest feelings. We have been talking about the language of art; it is really a language of feeling through visual images. We have said that not every visual image produces an immediate "wow" experience, especially new or puzzling works of art. Sometimes the "wow" comes from what we've been doing together in this book—talking about a sculpture one part at a time and putting it back together again, making connections between the artwork and the world around us. We move from our initial response to one that is informed by language, enlivened by a dialogue with art.

When a sculpture works, whether it causes a strong reaction or not, we feel it. We say the piece is unified if the content, materials, and elements of a sculpture come together to make a satisfactory whole. It leaves us feeling as if something is lacking if unity is not there. In the first chapter we turned a corner to discover *Batcolumn* (FIG. 49). We began asking questions. What makes it a sculpture? What does it mean? Let's look again at *Batcolumn* and several other by now familiar sculptures to see how the parts work as a whole.

This colossal baseball bat is made of Cor-Ten steel painted gray. By limiting the material and color of *Batcolumn*, Oldenburg holds the elements of the sculpture together. The steel beams form an interlaced pattern that give the piece a continuous rhythm. Each unit relates in basic shape, size, and color to the next. The use of this latticework design not only allows the surface to reflect the light but allows the light and surrounding space to come through.

Another way an artist seeks unity is by giving the parts a common direction. Echoing the tall buildings that compose Chicago's skyline, this vertical structure reaches up to the sky. We are reminded of the Eiffel Tower in Paris or the underpinnings of a building under construction. *Batcolumn* salutes a city proud of its progressive architecture, as well as its baseball teams. However, does this witty transformation of a baseball bat transcend its subject matter? Oldenburg's whimsical salute to baseball is more an homage than a joke or parody because of the strong impact of its simple, towering form. Perhaps the exaggerated size and the subject, an ordinary baseball bat, are meant to shock people into looking around them, into forming opinions about the condition of their city.

This process of transformation of the familiar to the unfamiliar is part of what commands our attention in a work of art. In John Chamberlain's compressed car sculpture it is the material that is transformed. The recognizable metallic sheen informs us at once that this crinkled, rusted

FIG. 49. Claes Oldenburg and Coosje van Bruggen, *Batcolumn*, 1977. Flat bar Cor-Ten steel, Cor-Ten tubing, and cast aluminum, painted gray. The sculpture is 100'8" high. The widest diameter is 9'9" and the narrowest is 4'6". The sculpture weighs 20 tons. Located on the Social Security Administration Building Plaza in Chicago.

**John Chamberlain in his studio, surrounded by the raw material of his sculptures.**
(Photo courtesy of The Pace Gallery)

form is made from automobile parts. The dented, scraped condition of the metal reminds us of junkyards, of the fact that old cars become by-products of an industrial society. We see them piled up or abandoned on roadsides all over America. To most Americans the car means freedom, power, and status. It also is a symbol for violence. We automatically make these associations; yet Chamberlain takes this "junk" material and recycles it into a compelling sculptural form. How does this transformation take place? The artist talked about the way he works and how he achieved a sense of unity in *Pure Drop* (FIG. 50) by experimenting as he went along.

Although the parts were painted, at the time I didn't like the way they looked. I figured we could make some adjustments. So I told the sandblaster to draw lines in them. It was interesting. Some days he was more impatient than others, so the lines got thicker. At first we sandblasted all the paint off one of the pieces to see if the metal surface was shiny. But it just went to matte . . .

THE SCULPTOR'S EYE

very gray. So we experimented some more and eventually came to the giraffelike skin.

We asked him why he wanted a shiny surface.

Glare. I wanted glare—an American tradition. The more glare the better. Fluff! Actually the color is a component of all the parts. Why is the paint job unfinished? Does it appear to be peeling? Then where it's peeling, it turns out to be the right amount of color. It might be matte or rusted, but it's also a linear drawing.

There's brightness. There's tone. Then there's the amount of color. If you put two colors together, there's never the same amount. I work in irregular slots. I fit one part to another part. In my studio, there's not one part that's the same. They have an irregular fit, and usually the color goes along with it. If it doesn't, I can always make adjustments. It works that way with chrome. If a piece looks heavy, bogged down, something like having an overstuffed stomach, a little chrome right down the creases gives relief.

**FIG. 50. John Chamberlain,** *Pure Drop*, **1983. Painted and chromium-plated steel, 135″ x 72″ x 36″.** Private Collection.

Louise Nevelson also was fascinated with abandoned junk. In *Sky Cathedral* (FIG. 51) one of the unifying features is that all the found objects placed in this series of boxes are cast-off bits of carpentry. The dominant shape is a square, the dominant color black. Variety within the theme is achieved by the smaller squares. In the compartments, cones, spheres, boxes, and other irregular forms are repeated in various sizes and configurations. Despite the variety of forms the whole is unified by repetition, by the overall texture (matte), the color (black), the material (wood), and the underlying grid pattern. Notice the play of light and dark, black on black, as the shadow of one form falls across another. The unifying color black not only emphasizes shadow and space but mystery. Some contrasting sensory words that come to mind are *muted/bold, simple/complex, curvilinear/straight, smooth/jagged, round/square, dark/light.*

FIG. 51. Louise Nevelson, *Sky Cathedral*, 1958. Assemblage: wood construction painted black, 11'3½" x 10'¼" x 18". The Museum of Modern Art, New York. Gift of Mr. and Mrs. Ben Mildwoff.

Like *Batcolumn*, *Study in Arcs* (FIG. 52) by David Smith moves the eye upward into space. These curved rods are suspended in motion, tossed into the air by some invisible hand. Time has stopped. The arcs are at the peak of their flight. There is a spontaneity to the lines, like a free-form gesture in paint. We sense a light touch in the repeated curves. By repeating patterns of shapes or lines, Smith unifies his composition. Again color fuses the parts into a whole. In this case, Smith emphasizes one color—pink—which allows us to enjoy the variety of dancing lines without being distracted. *Study in Arcs* is made of welded steel; yet the pink hue denies the toughness or hardness of the material. The effect is light, joyous. Although the sculpture is abstract and does not represent a recognizable image, we leap, like the arcs, into metaphor. The freedom of flight. The vigor of throwing something into the air and watching it in the moment before it falls to earth.

FIG. 52. David Smith, *Study in Arcs*, 1959. Steel painted pink, 132″ x 115½″ x 41½″. Storm King Art Center, Mountainville, New York. Gift of the Ralph E. Ogden Foundation.

We are reminded of the movement of branches bending in the spring breeze. We have pushed ourselves along through the flow of sensations and associations that *Study in Arcs* inspires. Our imaginations are challenged, our spirits lifted. The "wow" experience comes from saying, "Now I get it!" And our vision of the world expands, transformed by the sculptor's eye.

**A view of Storm King Art Center featuring *Momo Taro* by Isamu Noguchi.**
(Photo © Jerry L. Thompson)

# A FINAL NOTE

We saw *Study in Arcs* on a visit to Storm King Art Center one sunny but blustery afternoon in early spring. On the way back we talked excitedly about the works we had seen and interrupted ourselves to exclaim over the view out the car window. The late-afternoon sun made the bare branches of the woods next to the highway glow rose and mauve. The hillsides looked almost purple. Since we knew that David Smith had his studio not so very far away, we wondered if perhaps he too had seen the trees and branches glowing with color. Was the unusual pink hue of *Study in Arcs* his tribute to that rich and ruddy light? Writing about color, David Smith once said, "The April beauty of true color before it's struck with green." The artist might have been thinking of our rosy trees or a cherry orchard in full bloom or responding to some inner vision of his own. We had no way of knowing while driving down the highway. That didn't change our enjoyment in making the connection. One of the pleasures of art is that ultimately we, as viewers, find our own response to a work of art and our own references in daily life that we bring to art and that art enriches.

# ARTISTS' BIOGRAPHIES

At the end of each entry you will find the names of a few of the many museums where other works by these artists can be seen.

With the invention of photography in the 1840s, artists no longer needed to imitate reality. The use of an abstract form that did not represent or symbolize anything but itself was a twentieth-century innovation. American artists have been at the forefront of this movement, and after World War II their dynamic abstract paintings and sculpture placed the United States in the vanguard of art. Although American art displays a distinctive quality, it has its roots in the European tradition. The following paragraphs offer a brief overview of some of the movements that loosely classify the art presented in this book.

Surrealism, a European movement that explored dream imagery, influenced American artists such as David Smith, Isamu Noguchi, Alexander Calder, and Louise Bourgeois. These artists moved beyond Surrealism to create their own individual styles. Calder, for example, created mobiles of abstract shapes that hung from wires and moved with the slightest current of air. These works are called kinetic sculptures.

David Smith welded constructions out of found objects. He had an important impact on the next generation of American artists. They relied on intuition and spontaneity to create powerful works that were the sculptural equivalent of the paintings of the Abstract Expressionists. The compressed car sculptures of John Chamberlain and the abstract sculptures of Mark di Suvero, for example, demonstrate that abstract shapes made of throwaway materials can elicit strong emotional responses.

Reacting to the dominance of abstraction in painting and sculpture, a new group called Pop artists emerged in the late 1950s. Pop artists returned to realism and used everyday objects and images from our culture, including advertising and mass media. Robert Rauschenberg attached real objects to his canvases and included painting and silk screen in his sculpture so the boundaries between the two were blurred. The ironic sculptures of Claes Oldenburg often glorified food images or commonplace objects from telephones to typewriters to ice cream cones to baseball bats.

In the 60s a group of artists rejected the emotional works of the Abstract Expressionists and the realism of the Pop artists. Minimalist art, stressing the idea that the sculpture refers only to itself rather than to an outside meaning, is exemplified by the impersonal objects of Sol Le Witt or the fluorescent light sculptures of Dan Flavin. Minimalism is controlled, often fabricated at a factory or made of commercial materials, rather than "sculpted" by the hand of the artist. The form is spare, pared down. Conceptual art, which grew out of Minimalism, insists that the idea or concept of the work is more important than the finished product. Sometimes the ideas of conceptual art reduce the image to insignificance or abandon it entirely. Process art considers the art-making process. Richard Serra's sculpture is both minimal and process-oriented, but it defies categories. His Prop pieces in the 70s such as *One-Ton Prop* leave traces of the process that made them in that no attempt is made to disguise the rawness of the material or to embellish the surface.

Robert Smithson's large Earthworks, many of which no longer exist, emphasize a freedom from the commercialism and materialism so often associated with American culture. Earthworks, which depend on the use of the land and natural materials, are also referred to as site sculpture, as they are conceived for a specific site rather than placed in a museum or gallery. Beverly Pepper's *Cromlech Glen* reshapes the landscape and renews the viewer's responses to the natural environment. Site sculptures can also be made of other materials, such as steel or stone.

Although American art came into its own with Abstract Expressionism, American artists have consistently been concerned with realism, especially with the human form. George Segal's figures cast in plaster from live models evoke contemporary alienation of the human condition. Duane Hanson's superrealistic *Football Player* or Red Grooms's cartoonlike settings satirize contemporary American life.

Artists in the 80s and 90s continue to react to and reinvent the art of their predecessors. A preoccupation with realism, along with the underlying influences of abstraction, have forged an art that is both unique and innovative. New materials and technology, new ideas and developments, continue to inspire the imaginations and spirits of artists moving into the twenty-first century.

**BOURGEOIS, LOUISE.** Born 1911, Paris, France. She was educated at the Sorbonne, Ecole du Louvre, Ecole des Beaux-Arts, and other art schools in France. Her work includes painting and drawing, but she is primarily known for her sculpture and installations. She began to draw very young. Her parents had a business finding and restoring antique tapestries, and her first artwork was done for them. In 1938 she married an

American and moved to the United States, where she now lives. Look for the organic forms in her work.

Museum of Modern Art, New York; Whitney Museum of American Art, New York; Rhode Island School of Design, Providence; New York University.

**BUTTERFIELD, DEBORAH.** Born 1950, San Diego, California. She attended the University of California at Davis, where she received her B.F.A. Her early horses were made from scraps of wood, cast in bronze. More recently her assemblages of scrap-metal horses link memories of the American West with the present, and like John Chamberlain's sculptures proceed from the debris of our disposable culture.

Walker Art Center, Minneapolis; Metropolitan Museum of Art, New York; San Francisco Museum of Modern Art.

**CALDER, ALEXANDER.** Born 1898, Lawnton, Pennsylvania. Died 1976, New York City. His father and his grandfather were both artists. He received a B.S. in mechanical engineering, then attended the Art Students League in New York before going to France to study. There he developed the hanging wire sculptures named mobiles. His stationary cutout metal standing sculptures are called stabiles. He was the first American sculptor to achieve an international reputation.

Dallas Museum of Art; Metropolitan Museum of Art, New York; Musée National d'Art Moderne, Paris; Museum of Western Art, Moscow; Philadelphia Museum of Art.

**CHAMBERLAIN, JOHN.** Born 1927, Rochester, Indiana. He studied at the Art Institute of Chicago and Black Mountain College. The primary materials of his sculptures are automobile parts from old, junked, often rusting automobiles. His interest is in the forms, volumes, and color, but the cultural origin of the material cannot be overlooked. His work often is compared to the abstract expressionist or gestural painters such as Willem de Kooning or Franz Kline.

Museum of Modern Art, New York; Solomon R. Guggenheim Museum, New York; Tate Gallery, London; Galleria Nazionale d'Arte, Rome; Los Angeles County Museum of Art.

**DI SUVERO, MARK.** Born 1933, Shanghai, China. Mark di Suvero's father was in the Italian navy and was stationed in China when di Suvero was born there. When he was eight the whole family immigrated to the United States. He grew up in California, where he studied sculpture and philosophy at San Francisco City College, UCLA, and Berkeley. His bolted and welded constructions of wood and steel are considered the sculptural equivalent of the gestural brushstrokes of abstract expressionist paintings.

Wadsworth Atheneum, Hartford; Whitney Museum of American Art, New York; St. Louis Art Museum; Art Institute of Chicago; City of Toronto, Canada.

**FLAVIN, DAN.** Born 1933, Jamaica, New York. He studied at the U.S. Air Force Meteorological Technician Training School, the New School for Social Research, and Columbia University. His education didn't include any formal training in art; he began to take art seriously when he was twenty-six. One of the minimalists, the artist does not view his work, which usually is made up of fluorescent lights, as sculpture or painting and refers to them as "objects." To him, these objects demonstrate propositions or concepts about light, perception, and the definition of line and space.

National Gallery of Canada, Ottawa; Stedelijk Museum, Amsterdam; Norton Simon Museum of Art, Pasadena, California; Philip Johnson Collection, New Canaan, Connecticut; Dr. Peter Ludwig, Aachen, Germany.

**FREY, VIOLA.** Born 1933, Lodi, California. Studied at the California College of Arts and Crafts in Oakland and at Tulane University in New Orleans, where she received her M.F.A. Her glazed ceramic pieces originally were influenced by Japanese ceramics, but Viola Frey now uses bold overglazes and strong colors to manipulate volume and light in her work and to give a sense of movement to the surface. Look for large, colorful figures made from ceramic parts.

Redding Museum and Art Center, Connecticut; Fresno Art Museum, California; Laumeier Sculpture Park, St. Louis; Oakland Museum, Art Division.

**GRAVES, NANCY.** Born 1940, Pittsfield, Massachusetts. She received her B.A. degree from Vassar College and B.F.A. and M.F.A. from Yale University. Her early works were life-size camels in burlap, wood, and steel. Her painting, sculpture, and drawing has

**Nancy Graves at work.**
(Photo © Saff Tech Arts–George
Holzer. Courtesy of Nancy Graves)

been exhibited in the United States and Europe. She lived in Paris and later in Florence, but at present her studio is in New York City. Look for arrangements of recognizable objects combined into abstract forms.

Whitney Museum of American Art, New York; The Museum of Contemporary Art, Los Angeles; Art Institute of Chicago; The Museum of Fine Arts, Houston, Texas; National Gallery of Canada, Ottawa.

**GROOMS, RED.** Born 1937, Nashville, Tennessee. Studied at Peabody College, the New School for Social Research, the Chicago Art Institute School, and the Hofmann School in Provincetown, Massachusetts. Red Grooms is best known for exaggerated but realistic works such as *Rukus Manhattan*, complicated environments of figures and buildings that he assembles with the help of his Rukus Company, a group of artists working under his direction. These scenes vary from street scenes and the interior of a subway car with all the passengers, to a museum bookstore complete with guard.

Museum of Modern Art, New York; Art Institute of Chicago; Delaware Art Museum, Wilmington; Hirshhorn Museum and Sculpture Garden, Washington, D.C.; Moderna Museet, Stockholm.

**HANSON, DUANE.** Born 1925, Alexandria, Minnesota. He received his B.A. degree from Macalester College in St. Paul and then studied sculpture at Cranbrook Academy of Art in Bloomfield Hills, Michigan. He made several moves, but now lives in Florida. Hanson is best known for his extremely lifelike polyester resin figures, many of which are both social comments and witty satire. Check to be sure the next museum guard you see isn't a Hanson.

Milwaukee Art Museum; The Richmond Museum; Nelson-Atkins Museum of Art, Kansas City, Missouri; Neue Galerie, Aachen, Germany; Rotterdam Museum, The Netherlands.

**LE WITT, SOL.** Born 1928, Hartford, Connecticut. He graduated from Syracuse University and attended the School of Visual Arts in New York. He is a painter as well as a sculptor. His works are modular constructions manufactured at a factory. Some later works exist as a plan and a certificate from the artist, with a written description from which a wall drawing can be executed by the owner. Look for his spare white forms.

Art Gallery of Ontario, Toronto; Louisiana Sculpture Garden, Humlebaek, Denmark; Scottish National Gallery of Modern Art, Edinburgh; Los Angeles County Museum of Art; Kaiser Wilhelm Museum, Krefeld, Germany.

**LOVE, EDWARD A.** Born 1936, Los Angeles, California. Studied at California State University, received his B.F.A. and M.F.A. For more than twenty years Ed Love taught art at Howard University. He now teaches at Florida State University and is founding dean of the New World School of the Arts in Miami, Florida. Combining ancient African and modern American imagery, the twenty-seven painted rodlike figures, called The Arkestra, are inspired by famous black jazz and reggae musicians, many of whom he heard in clubs as a teenager growing up in L.A. His design projects have included public parks, theatrical sets and costumes, sound tracks, catalogues, exhibitions, and award-winning magazine art direction. He is also a performance and installation artist.

Howard University, Washington, D.C.; Goucher College, Baltimore; University of Massachusetts, Amherst; Golden State Life Insurance Company, Los Angeles; University of the District of Columbia, Washington, D.C.

**NEVELSON, LOUISE.** Born 1899, Kiev, Russia. Died New York City, 1988. Among other places she studied at the Art Students League in New York and the Hans Hoffman School in Munich. When she was six Louise Nevelson's family moved from Russia to Rockland, Maine. Her father owned a lumberyard, where she often played after school, making things from the scraps of wood. She studied drama, dance, and voice as well as art. This dramatic talent comes out in the sculpture for which she is best known, wooden wall reliefs in white, gold, or black.

Albright-Knox Art Gallery, Buffalo; Museum of Modern Art, New York; Art Institute of Chicago; Israel Museum, Jerusalem; Tate Gallery, London.

**NOGUCHI, ISAMU.** Born 1904, Los Angeles, California. Died 1988. He graduated from Columbia University, where he had gone to study medicine. He attended Leonardo da Vinci School in New York. Born in Los Angeles, he was four when his American mother took him to Japan. At thirteen his mother sent him by himself from Japan to Indiana to go to school there, and he did not return to Japan for many years. In 1942 he voluntarily spent a year interned with his fellow Japanese Americans in a camp in Arizona. Both his heritages, Japanese and Western, are part of his work. Talented in many mediums, he sculpted in stone, marble, metal and wood. He also made furniture and lighting and designed parks, playgrounds, and plazas, as well as stage sets. His former studio in Long Island City has been turned into a sculpture garden and museum for his work.

Metropolitan Museum of Art, New York; Cleveland Museum of Art; Academy of Art, Honolulu; Art Gallery of Ontario, Toronto.

**OLDENBURG, CLAES.** Born 1929, Stockholm, Sweden. He graduated from Yale University with a degree in English literature, and attended the Chicago Art Institute. When he was very young, he lived in Oslo and New York, but he grew up in Chicago. His works include large-scale objects made of muslin soaked in plaster and painted as well as soft sculptures made of vinyl or canvas painted and stuffed. He often makes the same object in several different sizes and mediums— for example, the ice-cream cone, one version of which appears in this book, also exists in several different sizes in painted plaster. He also is known for a series of monuments, some built and some only proposed. Since the early 70s he has worked in partnership with his wife, Dutch artist Coosje van Bruggen.

Vancouver Art Gallery, British Columbia; Museum of Modern Art, New York; Art Gallery of Ontario, Toronto; Art Institute of Chicago; Walker Art Center, Minneapolis.

**PEPPER, BEVERLY.** Born 1924, Brooklyn, New York. She studied industrial and advertising design at Pratt Institute, New York, the Art Students League, New York, and Atelier André L'Hôte, Paris. She worked for numerous advertising agencies in New York and later moved to Italy, where she has maintained residence since 1952. She paints but is primarily known as a sculptor. Her works are created in various mediums from highly polished stainless steel, to welded steel, to site-specific works including parks and playgrounds.

Fogg Art Museum, Cambridge, Massachusetts; Jacksonville Art Museum, Florida; Albright-Knox Art Gallery, Buffalo; Galleria d'Arte Moderna, Florence; Southland Mall, Memphis.

**PURYEAR, MARTIN.** Born 1941, Washington, D.C. He received his B.A. from Catholic University in Washington and then went to West Africa with the Peace Corps to teach art and biology. He attended the Swedish Academy of Art and received his M.F.A. from Yale University. He has taught at various universities and now lives in New York. His work includes monumental crafted outdoor pieces in wood. His work evokes the feelings of ancient cultures, dwellings, animal forms, and habitats—they are minimal yet crafted.

The Art Institute of Chicago; Metropolitan Museum of Art, New York; Philadelphia Museum of Art; Solomon R. Guggenheim Museum, New York; Joslyn Art Museum, Omaha.

**RAUSCHENBERG, ROBERT.** Born 1925, Port Arthur, Texas. After serving in the navy during World War II, he studied art at Kansas City Art Institute, the Académie Julian in Paris, Black Mountain College in North Carolina, and finally at the Art Students League in New York. Though he is a sculptor and a photographer, he is primarily known as a painter. Many of his works, like *Monogram*, are what he calls "combine" paintings, which combine found objects that exist in real space with the depicted space of painting and silk screens. These works blur the line between painting and sculpture.

Cornell University, Ithaca, New York; Tate Gallery, London; Whitney Museum of American Art, New York; Kaiser Wilhelm Museum, Krefeld, Germany; National Gallery of Canada, Ottawa.

**SEGAL, GEORGE.** Born 1924, New York, New York. He studied at Cooper Union for a year, Rutgers University part-time, and Pratt Institute before receiving a B.S. in art education at NYU. He got an M.F.A. from Rutgers in 1963. He grew up in New York, but after he received his education he went home to help his parents who had moved to New Jersey where they owned a chicken farm. There, in an abandoned henhouse, he gave up abstract painting and began to make plaster of paris casts of real people (at first using himself and his family as models) and grouping the lifelike sculptures in staged settings. He works in bronze as well as plaster. Some of his later works are painted, though not realistically.

Milwaukee Art Museum; San Francisco Museum of Modern Art; The Detroit Institute of Arts; St. Louis Art Museum; Hopkins Center Art Gallery, Dartmouth College, Hanover, New Hampshire; Des Moines Art Center, Iowa.

**SERRA, RICHARD.** Born 1939, San Francisco, California. He studied art in California and received a master's degree from Yale University. His early work shows an interest in the act or process of making art and the physical properties of the material. In Serra's prop series he explored themes of leaning and propped structure, balance, and repeating forms. His landscape-sited works command the viewer to move through and around them, changing our perception of the space.

Storm King Art Center, Mountainville, New York; Dallas Museum of Art; Allen Memorial Art Museum, Oberlin College, Ohio; Norton Simon Museum of Art, Pasadena, California; National Gallery of Canada, Ottawa; The Carnegie Museum of Art, Pittsburgh.

**SHAPIRO, JOEL.** Born 1941, New York, New York. He studied at New York University, where he received his B.A. and M.A. He introduced work in the 1970s that, unlike the large abstract sculpture popular at the time, was on a small scale and introduced recognizable objects—houses and blocky figures. His more recent pieces, figures with large rectangular limbs and torsos, have grown in scale. Simple and linear, these works—like Richard Serra's—explore a precarious sense of balance.

University of Massachusetts, Amherst; The Lannan Foundation, Palm Beach, Florida; Fogg Art Museum, Harvard University, Cambridge, Massachusetts; National Gallery of Australia, Cannaberra; Picker Art Gallery, Colgate University, Hamilton, New York; Cleveland Museum of Art; Museum of Modern Art, New York.

**SIMONDS, CHARLES.** Born 1945, New York, New York. He attended New Lincoln School, University of California at Berkeley, and Rutgers in New Jersey. The work in this book is one of hundreds of conceptual art pieces he made in the last twenty years that document an imaginary race of little people. Most of the works were built as temporary installations and were destroyed soon after their construction. He has written a history of the little people, a small book called *Three Peoples*, that traces the development of the culture and society of his invented civilization as it is reflected in his buildings and environments.

Centre National d'Art Contemporaire, Paris; Whitney Museum of American Art, New York; Allen Memorial Art Museum, Oberlin, Ohio; Massachusetts Institute of Technology, Cambridge; Centre Georges Pompidou, Paris.

**SMITH, DAVID.** Born 1906, Decatur, Indiana. Died 1965, Bennington, Vermont. He attended Cleveland Art School (correspondence course), graduated from Ohio University, then attended the Art Students League in New York. He may have received his most useful education at his summer job in the Studebaker automobile plant in South Bend, Indiana, where he learned to weld. He was one of the first sculptors in this country to use abstract welded and riveted metal forms, and to include found metal objects. Most of his works are in series. The works in this book are welded metal. Look for some of his other series grouped under the names *Tank Totem*, *Cubi*, and *Voltri*.

National Gallery of Art, Washington, D.C.; Dallas Museum of Art; Walker Art Center, Minneapolis; Metropolitan Museum of Art, New York; Los Angeles County Museum of Art.

**SMITHSON, ROBERT.** Born 1938, Passaic, New Jersey. Died 1973, Texas. He studied at the Art Students League in New York. His work is grouped under several different categories. *Spiral Jetty* is one of his earth-works, which reshape the natural environment. Included in his diverse body of work are gallery pieces consisting of rock specimens and collaged map drawings, essays on art, massive land pieces, and proposed projects for land reclamation. His pieces are concerned with ecological issues, a spiritual approach toward nature and art, and a rejection of commercialism.

Whitney Museum of American Art, New York; Milwaukee Art Museum; Neue Galerie, Aachen, Germany.

# GLOSSARY

Terms that relate to color and visual effects are grouped under these headings.

**abstract:** art in which the elements—line, shape, texture, or color—rather than a recognizable object have been stressed.

**abstract expressionism:** a style of art introduced by American artists in the 1940s and 50s in which color, line, shape, and/or texture is stressed rather than using a recognizable image to express emotion and meaning.

**aesthetic:** concerning the appreciation and perception of the formal and expressive qualities in art.

**archetype:** the original thing or example after which other things are modeled.

**assemblage:** a work of art that is assembled or made out of different nonart objects or materials, for example, *The Sweet Rockers* or *Sky Cathedral*.

**balance:** see **visual effects.**

**base:** the bottom part of a sculpture.

**biomorphic:** refers to a shape that looks as if it was reproduced from cells as life is reproduced.

**brass:** a mixture of copper and other metals, primarily zinc, used as a material, usually cast, in sculpture.

**bronze:** a mixture of copper and tin, used for casting in a mold.

**caricature:** a representation of a person or object in which features are exaggerated for purposes of humor or satire, for example, *Floor Cone* or *The Big Game*.

**cast: n.** a hollow mold from which a work of art can be made; **v.** the act of making a work of art from a hollow mold by pouring molten metal, liquid plaster, or other material into the mold and letting it harden.

**Celtic art:** art of the ancient and early medieval Celtic people in Europe or the British Isles.

**ceramics:** three-dimensional art made by shaping, firing to harden, and glazing clay, for example, *Me Man.*

**classical art:** art that emphasizes qualities considered to be characteristic of the Greek or Roman artistic spirit.

**color:** one of the elements of painting and sculpture: red, yellow, blue, green, orange, and violet, plus black or white and all their combinations.

   **hue:** another word for color; more technically it refers to the six pure colors.

   **primary colors:** red, yellow, and blue.

   **secondary colors:** orange, green, and violet.

   **complementary:** colors opposite each other on the color wheel, for example, red and green.

   **intensity:** the degree of strength or saturation of color.

   **value:** the lightness or darkness of a color.

**combine:** a form of assemblage in which real objects are combined with painted ones to form a work of art, for example, *Monogram.*

**common object:** ordinary objects of daily life, such as soup cans or lipsticks, that are the subjects of or the materials used in art.

**conceptual art:** in sculpture, art in which the idea or concept of the work is seen by the artist to be more important than the finished piece. For example, *Cubic Modular Piece No. 2.* The term is used to describe many kinds of art, including "performance art" and "happenings."

**contour:** the edge or boundary of a shape or form.

**Cor-Ten steel:** steel that needs no paint or other protective coating. Used for sculptures, it weathers to a rusty red-brown, for example, *One-Ton Prop*.

**diorama:** a small scenic model in which light is manipulated to achieve certain visual effects, often used in history museum exhibits; more generally a small three-dimensional scene.

**distortion:** to twist, pull or otherwise alter something out of its natural shape, for example, the figures in *Looking along Broadway towards Grace Church*.

**earthworks** or **earth art:** three-dimensional art made of or on the earth, usually noncommercial, which is to say not able to be bought or sold, often with environmental concerns, for example, *Spiral Jetty* or *Cromlech Glen*.

**elements:** the building blocks of art: color, shape, form, line, and texture.

**emphasis:** see **visual effects**.

**environment:** sculpture that creates a whole scene or tableau, for example, *The Red Light*.

**environmental art:** art that expresses environmental concerns, for example, *Spiral Jetty*.

**figurative/figural:** realistic or at least recognizable sculpture (or painting) of a human subject, landscape, or inanimate object, although also sometimes used to refer to art that concentrates specifically on the human figure, for example, *The Red Light* or *Football Player*.

**foreshorten:** an artistic device through which the proportions of objects, buildings, landscapes, or figures are changed to give the illusion of depth.

**form:** often used interchangeably with shape, but refers specifically to the three-dimensional quality or volume of a shape.

**found object:** an existing object found or selected by the artist and incorporated into a work of art, for example, *Sky Cathedral* or the goat in *Monogram*.

**frontal:** an artwork that is meant to be seen from one best point of view even though it may exist in the round, for example, *The Red Light*.

**grid:** a network of evenly spaced squares, flat or three-dimensional, used by many contemporary artists as a system for organizing their images, for example, *Cubic Modular Piece No. 2* and *Sky Cathedral*.

**harmony, harmonious:** refers to relationship of the parts of a sculpture; or the parts coming together in a pleasing way.

**hue:** the six pure colors—red, orange, yellow, green, blue, violet; see **color**.

**ideal:** refers to works of art that improve or perfect the appearance of nature.

**installation:** art that is built or installed in a specific room or area—can be temporary or permanent, for example, *Dwellings*.

**intensity:** see **color**.

**kinetic:** action or movement in a sculpture, whether through wind, gravity, or motor driven, for example, *Mother Peace* or the mobile *Indian Feathers*.

**maquette:** the French word for model, it has come to mean the small preliminary models sculptors make for their artworks; examples are in the photograph of artist Joel Shapiro.

**medium:** the material an artist choses to work in, whether oil paint, acrylic, bronze, or fabric.

**minimalist art:** art that relies on simple geometric

forms and the power of effect on the viewer with no intended personal references; see Dan Flavin's *Untitled*.

**mobile:** sculpture that moves, kinetic sculpture, often, but not necessarily; one that hangs suspended from the ceiling, for example, *Indian Feathers*.

**modeling:** building up or manipulating material such as clay or wax; the act of sitting for a painting or sculpture.

**monolith:** single large block of stone, usually vertical, for example, *Core*.

**multiple:** several identical or almost identical works of art by an artist, usually numbered, see, for example, *The Big Game*, which is one of five.

**niche:** a recess or indentation in a wall to contain a sculpture, for example, see *Dwellings, 1981*.

**nonobjective art:** refers to art in which color, shape, form, line, or texture is stressed without a recognizable image, for example, *Mother Peace* or *Study in Arcs*.

**organic:** having the physical structure characteristic of living organisms; or that which, even though inanimate, reminds us of a living form, for example, *Lever No. 3*.

painter puts paint on a surface, usually implying a brush loaded with paint, loosely and richly or "brushily" applied; also broken painted forms, not hard-edged forms. It also can refer to a painter's sensibility about a surface.

**pedestal:** structure a sculpture stands on that sets it apart from its surroundings.

**pop art:** the style of art in which the subject matter features images from popular culture—advertising, cartoons, commercial art, or common objects. For example, see *Floor Cone* and *Batcolumn*.

**primary colors:** red, yellow, and blue.

**principles of art:** another way of referring to visual effects or balance, emphasis, rhythm, space, unity, and variety.

**process art:** art in which the making of the work is stressed rather than the finished piece.

**proportion:** the relationship of the parts of a sculpture to one another and to the sculpture as a whole.

**real space:** actual space, as opposed to depicted space as in a painting.

**realistic art:** sculpture (or painting) with a recognizable subject that imitates life. For example, see *The Red Light*. Also see **superrealist sculpture**.

**relief:** originally used to describe sculptural forms that projected from a fixed background, usually carved, but now used more broadly to describe works that are three-dimensional but hang on a wall, for example, *The Big Game*, or that stand against a wall, for example, *Sky Cathedral*.

**repetition:** see **visual effects**.

**rhythm:** see **visual effects**.

**round/in the round:** the ability of a work of art to be viewed from all sides, for example, *Batcolumn*.

**series:** a group of works by an artist that explore a theme or materials in a variety of ways. For example, see *Lever # 1* and *Lever No. 3*.

**shape:** one of the elements of sculpture and painting.

**silk-screen process:** a stenciled process of color reproduction, often using photographs.

**site specific:** a work made for a particular place or "site," usually, though not always, out of doors.

**soft sculpture:** refers to art made from substances such as cloth or vinyl rather than the more durable hard materials associated with sculpture, for example, *Floor Cone.*

**stabiles:** a word coined to describe the standing biomorphic sculptures of Alexander Calder.

**style:** characteristic manner or appearance of works of individual artists, groups of artists who work in a related way (schools), or periods of art.

**superrealist sculpture:** style of art in which objects, people, or places are presented in a highly realistic form. For example, see *Football Player.*

**symmetry/symmetrical:** visually evenly balanced, both sides being equal or the same; also see **visual effects.**

**tableau:** people or objects arranged to suggest a scene or a moment frozen in time, used to describe some environments, for example, *The Red Light.*

**taxidermy:** the art of preparing and mounting the skin of dead animals or fish to make them appear lifelike.

**three-dimensional:** having, or appearing to have, length, width, and depth.

**unity:** see **visual effects.**

**value:** the darkness (black or some dark color added to a pure hue) or lightness (white or some light color added to a pure hue) of a color; also, the darkness or lightness of a shape, form, or even a whole sculpture or painting.

**variety:** see **visual effects.**

**visual effects:** the principles of design by which the elements in a sculpture or painting are arranged. Compositional devices, among them, balance, emphasis, rhythm, variety, space, and unity.

> **balance: formal** balance refers to the **symmetrical** arrangement of the elements of a work of art; **informal** balance to the **asymmetrical** arrangement of the elements. The human eye seems to have an inborn ability to tell when something is balanced or in equilibrium—sculptors often intentionally play with this sense.
>
> **emphasis:** the element that is stressed or most prominent in a work of art.
>
> **rhythm:** movement is suggested by repeating elements in visual patterns—for example, the **repetition** of a shape or a color in a work of art to create an effect, or the **alternating** of a shape with another shape or shapes to the same end.
>
> **variety:** the many elements or the diversity of one element within a work of art, for example, a number of different shapes or colors to provide contrast and visual interest.
>
> **unity:** the harmonious or visually satisfying blending of all of the visual effects in a work of art; all the parts relate to the whole.

**volume:** the three-dimensional quality of a form or shape.

**welded constructions:** art in which the sculpture is built by an artist using a welding torch to attach metal parts to each other. For examples, see *Hudson River Landscape, Fallen Sky, Tanz.*

**welding:** the process of attaching metal parts of a sculpture to one another by melting or braising with a torch.

# LIST OF SCULPTURES

Louise Bourgeois, *Décontractée*, 1990. Pink marble & steel, 28½" × 36" × 23" overall. (Photo by Peter Bellamy. Courtesy of the Robert Miller Gallery.)

Deborah Butterfield, *Horse*, 1985. Construction of painted and rusted sheet steel, wire and steel tubing, 82⅛" × 118⅝" × 34¼". Hirshhorn Museum and Sculpture Garden, Smithsonian Institution, Washington, D.C. The Thomas M. Evans, Jerome L. Green, Joseph H. Hirshhorn, and Sydney and Frances Lewis Purchase Fund. (Photo by Lee Stalsworth.)

Alexander Calder, *Indian Feathers*, 1969. Painted aluminum sheet and stainless steel rods, 136¾" × 91" × 63". Whitney Museum of American Art, New York. Purchase with funds from the Howard and Jean Lipman Foundation, Inc. (Photo by Jerry L. Thompson.)

John Chamberlain, *Pure Drop*, 1983. Painted and chromium-plated steel, 135" × 72" × 36". Private Collection. (Photo courtesy of The Pace Gallery.)

Mark di Suvero, *Mother Peace*, 1970. Steel painted red-orange, 39'6" high. Storm King Art Center, Mountainville, New York. Gift of the Ralph E. Ogden Foundation. (Photo by Jerry L. Thompson. Photo of details by Linda Steigleder.)

Dan Flavin, *Untitled*, 1987. Fluorescent lights, 48" × 48", Greenberg Gallery, St. Louis. (Photo courtesy of Greenberg Gallery.)

Viola Frey, *Double Grandmother*, 1978–79. Glazed white clay, 61½" high. Minneapolis Institute of Arts. Gift of the Regis Corporation. (Photo © Minneapolis Institute of Arts.)

—*Me Man*, 1983. Glazed ceramic, 99" × 29¾" × 25". Whitney Museum of American Art, New York. Gift of William S. Bartman. (Photo by Geoffrey Clements.)

Nancy Graves, *Tanz*, 1984 (glass series). Bronze with baked enamel, 19" × 19½" × 10". Collection of Ann and Robert Freedman, New York. © Nancy Graves/ VAGA NY 1993. (Photo by Ken Cohen.)

—*Harvester K.C.*, 1986. Stainless steel and bronze with polyurethane paint, 18' × 8' × 14'. Courtesy of United Missouri Bank Collection, Kansas City, Missouri. © Nancy Graves/VAGA NY 1993. (Photo courtesy of Nancy Graves.)

Red Grooms, *Looking along Broadway towards Grace Church*, 1981. Alkyd paint, gator board, Celastic, wood, wax, foam core, 180.3 cm × 161.9 cm × 73 cm. (70¼" × 63¼" × 28½"). Cleveland Museum of Art. Gift of Agnes Gund in honor of Edward Henning. © Red Grooms/ARS NY. (Photo © Cleveland Museum of Art.)

—*The Big Game*, 1980. Painted cast aluminum, 96" × 101" × 17", edition of three. Courtesy of United Missouri Bank Collection, Kansas City, Missouri. © Red Grooms/ARS NY. (Photo © United Missouri Bank Collection.)

Duane Hanson, *Football Player*, 1981. Oil on polyvinyl,

43¼″ × 30″ × 31½″, Lowe Art Museum, University of Miami, Coral Gables, Florida. Museum purchase through funds from the Friends of Art and public subscription. (Photo © Lowe Art Museum.)

Sol Le Witt, *Cubic Modular Piece No. 2 (L-Shaped Modular Piece)*, 1966. Baked enamel on steel, 109⅛″ × 57⅞″ × 59⅞″. Walker Art Center, Minneapolis. Art Center Acquisition Fund. (Photo © Walker Art Center.)

—*Five Towers*, 1986. Painted wood, 8 units, overall: 86⁹⁄₁₆″ × 86⁹⁄₁₆″ × 86⁹⁄₁₆″. Whitney Museum of American Art, New York. Purchase with funds from the Louis and Bessie Adler Foundation, Inc. (Seymour M. Klein, President), the John I. H. Baur Purchase Fund, the Grace Belt Endowed Purchase Fund, the Sondra and Charles Gilman, Jr., Foundation, Inc., the List Purchase Fund, and the Painting and Sculpture Committee. (Photo by Geoffrey Clements.)

Ed Love, *The Sweet Rockers*, 1988 (from the Arkestra). Welded steel, paint, mixed media; height 68″ to 82″. Collection of the artist. (Photo by Jennifer Verdenk.)

Louise Nevelson, *Sky Cathedral*, 1958. Assemblage: wood construction painted black, 11′3½″ × 10′1¼″ × 18″. Museum of Modern Art, New York. Gift of Mr. and Mrs. Ben Mildwoff. (Photograph © 1992 The Museum of Modern Art, New York.)

Isamu Noguchi, *Core (Cored Sculpture)*, 1978. Basalt, 74″. Isamu Noguchi Garden Museum, Long Island City, New York. (Photo by Michio Noguchi, courtesy of the Isamu Noguchi Foundation, Inc.)

—*Momo Taro*, 1977. Granite, nine pieces, 9′ × 35′2″ × 22′8″. Storm King Art Center, Mountainville, New York. Purchase. (Photo by Jerry L. Thompson.)

Claes Oldenburg, *Floor Cone (Giant Ice-Cream Cone)*, 1962. Synthetic polymer paint on canvas filled with foam rubber and cardboard boxes, 53¾″ × 11′4″ × 56″. The Museum of Modern Art, New York. Gift of Philip Johnson. (Photograph © 1992 The Museum of Modern Art, New York.)

Claes Oldenburg and Coosje van Bruggen, *Batcolumn*, 1977. 24 verticals and 1,608 connecting units of ⅝″ × 3″ flat bar Cor-Ten steel. The inner structure is made of 2″ Cor-Ten tubing. The knob is made of 24 sections of cast aluminum welded together. The sculpture is 100′8″ high. The widest diameter is 9′9″ and the narrowest is 4′6″. The sculpture weighs 20 tons. Located on the Social Security Administration Building Plaza in Chicago. (Photograph courtesy of Claes Oldenburg and Coosje van Bruggen.)

Beverly Pepper, *Cromlech Glen*, 1985–90. Rock, earth, evergreen trees, sod, flagstones, 25′ × 130′ × 90′. Laumeier Sculpture Park, St. Louis. (Photo by Robert La Rouche.)

—*Fallen Sky*, 1968. Stainless steel and baked enamel, 105″ × 181″ × 58″. Hirshhorn Museum and Sculpture Garden, Smithsonian Institution, Washington, D.C. (Photo courtesy of Beverly Pepper.)

Martin Puryear, *Lever #1*, 1988. Red cedar, 429.3 cm × 340.4 cm × 45.7 cm. (167½" × 132¾" × 17¾"). The Art Institute of Chicago, the A. James Speyer Memorial, with additional funds provided by UNR Industries in honor of James W. Alsdorf, Barbara Neff and Solomon Byron Smith Funds. (Photo by Thomas Cinoman.)

—*Lever No. 3*, 1989. Carved and painted wood, 84½" × 162" × 13". National Gallery of Art, Washington, D.C. Gift of the Collectors Committee. (Photo © National Gallery of Art.)

Robert Rauschenberg, *Monogram*, 1955–59. Stuffed goat, tire, mixed media, and canvas, 64" × 63" × 37". Statens Konstmuseer, Stockholm, Sweden. © Robert Rauschenberg/VAGA NY 1993. (Photo © Statens Konstmuseer.)

George Segal, *The Red Light*, 1972. Plaster, mixed media, 114" × 96" × 36". Cleveland Museum of Art. Andrew R. and Martha Holden Jennings Fund. © George Sega/NAGA NY 1993. (Photo © Cleveland Museum of Art.)

—*Trapeze*, 1971. Plaster, rope, metal and wood, 72" × 36". Wadsworth Atheneum, Hartford. Gift of Joseph L. Schulman and an anonymous donor. © George Segal/VAGA NY 1993. (Photo © Wadsworth Atheneum.)

Richard Serra, *One-Ton Prop (House of Cards)*, 1969. Lead antimony, 4 plates, each 48" × 48" × 1". The Museum of Modern Art, New York. Gift of the Grinstein Family. (Photo by Dorothy Zeidman, courtesy of the Leo Castelli Gallery.)

Joel Shapiro, *Untitled, 1984.* Bronze, 203.2 cm × 200.7 cm × 99.1 cm. (79¼" × 78¼" × 38¾"). St. Louis Art Museum. Gift of Mr. and Mrs. Barney A. Ebsworth. (Photo © St. Louis Art Museum.) (Photos on page 47 taken outdoors during an exhibit at the Baltimore Museum of Art, photos courtesy of the St. Louis Art Museum.)

—*House on a Field*, 1975–77. Bronze with a wooden base, 21" × 21¾" × 28¾" × 2". Private Collection.

Charles Simonds, *Dwellings, 1981* (detail, four of eight panels). Unfired clay wall relief, 96" × 528". Museum of Contemporary Art, Chicago. Gift of Douglas and Carol Cohen. (Photo © Museum of Contemporary Art.)

David Smith, *Hudson River Landscape*, 1951. Welded steel, 49½" × 75" × 16¾". Whitney Museum of American Art, New York, purchase. © David Smith/VAGA NY 1993. (Photo by Jerry L. Thompson.)

—*Study in Arcs*, 1959. Steel painted pink, 132" × 115½" × 41½". Storm King Art Center, Mountainville, New York. Gift of the Ralph E. Ogden Foundation. © David Smith/VAGA NY 1993. (Photo by Jerry L. Thompson.)

Robert Smithson, *Spiral Jetty*, 1970. Black basalt and limestone rocks and earth, 1,500 feet. Great Salt Lake, Utah. Estate of the artist. (Photo by Gianfranco Gorgoni.)

# SCULPTURE PARKS AND GARDENS

Brookgreen Gardens, Murrells Inlet, South Carolina (figurative art)

California Scenario, Costa Mesa, California (an environment and sculpture garden in the middle of a town, designed and executed by Isamu Noguchi)

Dallas Museum of Art, Texas

Hirshhorn Museum and Sculpture Garden, Washington, D.C.

Laumeier Sculpture Park and Museum, St. Louis, Missouri

Nathan S. Manilow Park, University Park, Illinois

Metropolitan Museum of Art Roof Garden, New York, New York

Museum of Modern Art Garden, New York, New York

Franklin D. Murphy Sculpture Garden at UCLA, Los Angeles, California

Nelson-Atkins Museum of Art, Kansas City, Missouri

Isamu Noguchi Garden Museum, Long Island City, New York

Oakland Museum, California

Pepsico Sculpture Gardens, Purchase, New York

A view of *Public Goddess*, 1992, by Judith Shea at Laumeier Sculpture Park in St. Louis. (Photo © Laumeier Sculpture Park)

John B. Putnam, Jr., Memorial Collection at Princeton University, New Jersey

Storm King Art Center, Mountainville, New York

Whitney Museum Sculpture Court at Philip Morris, New York, New York

Walker Art Center Sculpture Garden, Minneapolis, Minnesota

# BIBLIOGRAPHY

Arnason, H. H. *History of Modern Art*, 3rd ed. Revised and updated by Daniel Wheeler. New York: Harry N. Abrams, Inc., 1986.

Atkins, Robert. *ArtSpeak: A Guide to Contemporary Ideas, Movements, and Buzzwords*. New York: Abbeville Press, 1990.

Baigell, Matthew. *Dictionary of American Art*. New York: Harper and Row, 1979.

Beardsley, John. *Earthworks and Beyond: Contemporary Art in the Landscape*. New York: Abbeville Press, 1989.

Berger, John. *About Looking*. New York: Pantheon Books, 1980.

Broudy, Harry S. *The Role of Imagery in Learning*. Los Angeles: The Getty Center for Education in the Arts, 1987.

Burnham, Jack. *Beyond Modern Sculpture: The Effects of Science and Technology on the Sculpture of this Century*. New York: George Braziller, 1968.

———*The Structure of Art* (rev. ed.). New York: George Braziller, 1973.

Craig, Martin, and Others. *Minimalism* (Exhibition). Tate Gallery, Liverpool. Alan Dock, Liverpool, 1989.

Feldman, Edmund Burke: *Varieties of Visual Experience: Art as Image and Idea*. Englewood Cliffs, N.J.: Prentice-Hall, Inc., 1967; Rev. and enlarged ed., New York: H. N. Abrams, 1972.

Hunter, Sam. *American Art of the 20th Century*. New York: Harry N. Abrams, Inc., 1972.

Krauss, Rosalind E. *The Originality of the Avant-Garde and Other Modernist Myths*. Cambridge, Massachusetts, and London, England: The MIT Press, 1985.

———*Passages in Modern Sculpture*. Cambridge, Massachusetts, and London, England: The MIT Press. 1977: also New York: Viking, 1977.

———*Richard Serra/Sculpture*. New York: The Museum of Modern Art, 1986.

Lawrence, Sidney. *Music in Stone: Great Sculpture Gardens of the World*. A Train/Branca Book. New York: Scala Books, 1984.

Lippard, Lucy R. *Pop Art* (with contributions by Lawrence Alloway, Nancy Marmer, Nicolas Calas). London: Thames and Hudson Ltd., 1966; also New York: Praeger, 1966.

Lucie-Smith, Edward. *Art Now*. New York: William Morrow, 1977. Secaucus, New Jersey: The Wellfleet Press, 1989.

Parsons, Michael J. *How We Understand Art: A Cognitive Developmental Account of Aesthetic Experience*. Cambridge/New York: Cambridge University Press, 1987.

Pincus-Witten, Robert. *Bourgeois Truth*. New York: Robert Miller Gallery, 1982.

Ragens, Rosalind. *ArtTalk*. Encino, Calif.: Glencoe Publishing Co., 1988.

Rauschenberg, Robert. *Rauschenberg*: Elizabeth Avedon Editions: An Interview with Barbara Rose. New York: Vintage Books, 1987.

Rose, Barbara. *Claes Oldenburg*. New York: The Museum of Modern Art and the New York Graphic Society, 1969.

Russell, John. *The Meanings of Modern Art*. New York: Harper and Row, 1981.

Sims, Patterson. *Whitney Museum of American Art Catalogue*. New York: Whitney Museum of American Art in association with W. W. Norton, 1985.

*David Smith by David Smith: Sculpture and Writings*. Cleve Gray, ed. London and New York: Thames and Hudson, 1968.

Stitch, Sidra. *Made in the U.S.A.: An Americanization in Modern Art: The 50's and 60's*. Berkeley and Los Angeles: University of California Press, 1987.

Tomkins, Calvin. *Post- to- Neo: The Art World of the 1980's*. New York: Henry Holt Company, Inc., 1988.

*Walker Art Center: Painting and Sculpture from the Collection*. Museum Catalog, Minneapolis and New York: Walker Art Center and Rizzoli International Publications, Inc., 1990.

# INDEX

## ABOUT THE AUTHORS

JAN GREENBERG is a writer, teacher, and art educator who directed the Aesthetic Education Master of Arts in Teaching program at Webster University in St. Louis. She is also the author of a number of books for young readers. She lives in St. Louis.

SANDRA JORDAN is a writer and photographer. For many years she was an editor of books for young readers. She and Jan Greenberg are the coauthors of *The Painter's Eye: Learning to Look at Contemporary American Art*. She grew up in Cleveland and now lives in New York City.